FAR BEYOND
THE DEAD END

By the same author

Something in Your Eyes

FAR BEYOND
THE DEAD END

Saikat Baksi

Srishti
PUBLISHERS & DISTRIBUTORS

SRISHTI PUBLISHERS & DISTRIBUTORS
N-16, C. R. Park
New Delhi 110 019
editorial@srishtipublishers.com

First published by
Srishti Publishers & Distributors in 2014

Typeset by Eshu Graphic

*Dedicated to the past that grows younger
with every passing moment...*

AMONG THE RUINS

He stood rooted to the spot gazing at the battered pile of bricks. He had known them for eternity. They had existed in his life for countless years…perhaps more than a millennium. Yet, they were overlooked. The red bricks appeared rather whitish under the generous flash of full moon. The uneven wrinkled surface seemed to smirk at him, "Who am I?" He wanted to touch it. Perhaps a touch would open the floodgates. A rush of the forgotten past would wash out all the blockades. He would instantly see what lay beyond that opaque wall of oblivion.

Slowly, he approached a brick that hung loose at the edge of the wall. Grabbing it, he gave a slight jerk. The brick came out of its primordial socket. He held it near his eyes to look for a clue.

"Put that down, right now!"

The roaring dictate jolted him, and the brick slipped from his shaking hand.

"How dare you destroy that antiquity?" Another volley of thunderous reproach rocked him. He swung around in panic. The entire place was deserted. He never realized the pulse of a single living creature among the ruins. Then who had emerged from this haze of nothingness?

Suddenly his eyes fell on a tall robust figure of an old man cloaked in a white robe. The glaring eyes seized him with cold rage. After a brief spell of blankness, he mumbled, "Who are you? I never saw anyone here."

"Who am I? Good question! I am not surprised that fools like you never paid attention to my voice for thousands of years. I am Aristobulus, the Army General of the Alexander the Great. I am the first one to notice these ruins. But, nobody paid any heed to me."

He retreated a few steps. The unreal demeanor seemed to tower menacingly over his terrified existence. "I am sorry for invading your privacy. But what are you doing here? This is twentieth century. Alexander came to this land almost two and half millennia ago!"

"Yes! I am guarding the testimony of a great civilization. Nobody seems to bother to save it. Idiots like you destroy these remains bit by bit."

"He is not alone! Even I described thousands of such deserted villages in great detail. No one bothered." Another voice boomed from behind the wall. One more figure, like a wavering shadow, emerged from the darkness. "I am Strabo the historian. I visited this place five hundred years after Aristobulus."

He was gripped by terror and bafflement. Words failed to come forth in his dry mouth.

A third shadow swayed along the sinister alley, "I am still repenting for almost a century that I took away so many of these bricks for making that bloody railway track between Multan and Lahore. But what could I do? I was not an archeologist. The locals told me that there was a large pile of bricks nearby. I never found stones to lay the foundation of the railway tracks. So I got the bricks from there. I had no clue about its antiquity. I am guarding these ancient remains for more than a decade now. You cannot cause any more damage to it." The ethereal image of the stout and tall gentleman in formal British attire spoke in a tone of penitence.

"William Brunton!" He uttered in a hypnotic trance, "But none of you are alive!"

All three of them started to close in around him. He wanted to turn and run away but was blocked by the ancient walls. In a few moments, three towering figures were standing next to him. He could almost feel their breath. In a fit of terror, he tried to scream; but nothing came out of his mouth.

"We don't pardon trace passers. We bury them, right here, under these ill-fated ruins." The inviolable dictate resounded like an eternal verdict.

Seized by panic, he felt the ground sinking beneath his feet; the walls shaking; the bricks falling loose one after the other. He tried to move, but could not. Half of his body had disappeared below layers of soil. "They are waiting for you for more than three thousand years. Join them. Good bye!" Three voices spoke in unison.

He made a final desperate attempt to scream but a large brick came flying to hit his face.

He sat up on his make-shift bed with a jolt, soaked in perspiration. The rush of labored breathing slowed down a bit. "It was just a nightmare!" He felt relaxed. "There could not be any Aristobulus, Strabo or Branton to bury him under the rubble. He removed the bed sheet and got up from the bed with a parched throat. Picking up the bottle of water from the corner of the tent, he gulped half of it in a hurry. The eyes were still veiled with a layer of the disturbing dream. He pulled aside the curtain of the tent and stepped outside. The full moon vanished with his dream. The entire ruin was painted with impregnable darkness. He went back and gathered the torch.

A splash of water felt good and almost washed off the haze. Suddenly, a rustling noise from a distance caught his attention and he flashed the torch in that direction. From behind the watery layer, he saw a human figure swiftly moving along the dilapidated wall. He rubbed his eyes and yelled, "Hey…who is that?"

The figure scrambled and disappeared behind the dark pile of bricks. He started chasing. In a moment he was on the other side of the wall. The figure moved in a rapid pace along the burnt brick lane between the ancient walls. The bright flash of torch followed the figure. He shouted again, "Stop there…"

The figure dashed along the alley in manic frenzy. Suddenly, a pile of debris came on its way, and it stumbled. The figure tripped and collapsed on the ground with a grunt. In a moment, he was standing above a young man wrapped in a blanket. He yanked away the blanket and flashed the light straight on the man's face. "Who are you? What are you doing here?" He demanded.

The man squinted under the glare of the torch and folded his hand, "Please let me go, sir. I am just a poor man. The villagers say that this place is very old; and there are lots of precious stones hidden underground. Since you people started digging this place, I have been hunting for those jewels. If I get a few, my life would be better. I am a very poor man sir."

"Did you find any? Tell me the truth. This excavation is being done under the mandate of the Government. Nothing can be taken away from here. If you are caught stealing even a brick from this site, you will be put behind bars."

The man pleaded, "Sir, I got some of these red stones, also a few golden beads. But, I don't have money to eat two meals a day. Don't take this away from me." The man delved in his pocket and stretched out his hand. A couple of stones and golden beads sparkled under the white glaze of torchlight.

He looked at them for a moment in puzzlement. "Where did you find them?"

The man pointed his finger at a row of decrepit barracks just excavated the day before. He thought for a moment and grabbed the man by the neck, "Come with me. Let me call my colleagues also. Show us the places where you found these. I shall let you keep these few stones, but you must cooperate with us."

After an hour, the man was seated by a fire, surrounded by a group of archeologists.

"How old is this place?" asked one of them.

"The folklore says it is older than that stupa." The thief sounded eager to oblige the captors with information.

"Which stupa? The one out there with round dome?"

"Yes. There used to be monks living there once upon a time. But long before the monks came, this place was a vibrant town. That's what the elders think." The thief was glad that he was able to feed their curiosity.

"Where have they gone?"

"We don't know. Nobody had ever seen the monks. They say that there are heaps of dead-bodies buried right here, below this ground. Villagers have seen ghostly shadows hovering over this place at night. That's why we call it Mohenjo-Daro. It means the mound of the dead," said the thief.

"You are not scared, it seems!"

The thief looked slightly embarrassed. After a brief pause, he said, "Everyone knows that there are treasures hidden under the soil here. Even the stupa had plenty. Over a period of time, the villagers had taken away most of it. But, this place was beyond reach until it was dug."

"Hmm…but you people can't touch a thing now. It is under the control of the Government."

The thief laughed nervously. A trace of sarcasm fleeted across his face, "I understood that, but you see, most of the houses over there are built by these bricks. Such massive piles of burnt bricks were totally unclaimed all these years. Perhaps, the owners had been sleeping below many layers of soil! Until you guys arrived, it was free for all."

"We can understand. But now it is against law, and we can hand you over to the police. We shall not do so provided you show us the exact spot where you found those gems tomorrow morning."

"I shall show you. There may be many more all over that lane between the barracks. I could not see in the dark. What are you going to do with such stones? The villagers can live a better life if they have it."

"They are extremely precious."

"I know. But you people seem to be some kind of scholars. You don't need much money."

"These are far beyond money. Can you get your childhood back?"

The thief laughed, "I don't want it back! Of course, even if I want, I shall not get it."

"Each object among this debris is holding some irrevocable past in its cradle. Money cannot buy that."

The thief stared at them blankly for a long moment, "Well, I am just a thief. I don't understand much of what you say. I shall show you the places."

The group of archeologists dispersed.

The next day, the first thing in the morning, they would have to explore the place meticulously. Apparently, this was the lower town of the ancient settlement. The line of barracks was evidently inhabited by the poor of the society. How could a hoard of jewels land here? What brought such riches to this part of the town?

ONE EVENING...THREE MILLENNIA AGO...

1

The dark shadow moved on the sly under the pendulous branches of the Deodar tree. A light breeze swept over the dense foliage, and a few pointed leaves tickled his neck. His obsessive stalking was hindered. He whacked away at the hanging leaves. The trees were not full grown in this part of the riverbank. Weather had turned quirky over the years. The capricious river ran amok at wild fancy. Often it raided the elevated mud-brick platform and swept every bit of human settlement away in savage ferocity. Yet, the rich and powerful of the society lived in this area.

"These people don't seem to care about the impending peril!" He wondered. Well... it suited him now. He adjusted his posture hiding behind a thick bunch of leaves, and managed a clear view of the events in the house before him.

The vulnerable flame of the candle wavered at the stroke of a light wind. Koli picked up the candle, guarding its dancing flame with her palm and placed it in another corner of the room where the wind could not reach it. As she walked with the candle in her hand, he caught a glimpse of her silhouette. Raging lust flared up, and he ogled at the dark profile swaying slightly under the weight of a curvaceous bust. He clutched the tree trunk fiercely as if he could grab at the curvy flesh.

"Father says you have some extraordinary talent." Koli addressed the frail young man seated in one corner on a wooden stool.

"I don't know. If he says so, certainly I have. But finally, I must earn my living. This is my only concern right now. I cannot live forever in this house at his expense," said Sindhu.

"Don't bother much about it. Father will do something for you. He has excellent connections at the council. In fact, the ruler holds him with high regard. Without my father's approval, not a single seal gets the council's nod." Koli said with proud conviction and settled onto the bed across from Sindhu.

From behind the bunch of leaves, the shadowy figure watched Koli straight through the window. The shimmering glow danced on the gorgeous bearing, exploring her impudent sensuality. Wide eyed, he drank the image hungrily, inflamed with desire.

Sindhu traced the surface of a burnt-clay pot with his fingers and felt curious. He mumbled thoughtfully, "This is not common. Where did you get this?"

Koli feigned curiosity. "What's abnormal about that? That's another fired clay pot. You can find this all over our land."

Sindhu studied the design closely and after a long silence uttered an evasive answer. "No ... nothing."

From the furtive expression, Koli understood that Sindhu was suppressing something. She pressed, "No, you must tell me what bothered you about the pot. I bought it last month from the local market. I don't see anything remarkable in it!" Koli said with a muffled smile.

Sindhu hesitated a bit and then said, "The design is uncommon. In fact, the painting on the surface is truly exceptional. It's not another set of jagged lines or large-eyed fishes or a humped bull.

I am wondering who took the liberty to deviate from the grand heritage. I admire the artist who thought differently."

Koli was now smiling broadly. "Is that a good design?" She asked coyly.

Sindhu surveyed the surface once more with a critical eye and finally made his assessment. "Yes…it is indeed praiseworthy, but I appreciate the boldness to break the monotonous tradition more than the quality of work. I hate conventions you know; it kills every seed of development. Unless we venture forth upon the uncharted territory, we shall never discover a new place. Bending the rules is essential to move a few steps ahead of our predecessors."

"Well, the commonality is holding the empire together; otherwise it would have disintegrated long back. Consider the wide spread of race and creed living in this society. If everyone pulls a cart from all directions, it would never move!" Koli argued.

"Huh, this is your father's opinion. That's the trouble. We stopped indulging our own thought. We think only what has already been thought in the past." Sindhu spoke out in frustration.

"Whatever it is, but you admire the pot; I mean the person who conceived that unusual design." Koli said impishly.

"Yes, I do," declared Sindhu firmly.

"Well…I made it! It is not purchased from the market!" Koli burst into a convulsive laughter.

Bewildered, Sindhu looked at her, "Really?"

After a long moment, Sindhu said incredulously, "You did it! And you have been arguing with me in favor of conventions, whereas your own ideas are quite unorthodox. I am sure, you share my views. By the way, what else are you interested in?"

Koli waved her hand in dismissal, "Everything or nothing; my area of interest spans from talking to the peacocks to counting the stars. Well… Clay modeling and sculpting also fall somewhere inside this wide range! Only I am confused, for which of my skills should I ask for a commission from the council?" Koli said jocularly.

"At least three dozen successful craftsmen have been groomed under my guidance, but I failed to train my daughter!" The old man entered the room with a broad grin on his face. An upright bearing, straight like an arrow, rendered him distinguishable among the common crowd. Unlike most others, he had not acquired a plump tummy. A pair of narrow misty eyes appeared to be lost in thought all the time. The most striking feature on his face was his thin lips. Pouty thick lips were a regular feature among the people. Only the complexion did not betray his age and was a bit pale. The voice remained vibrant and virile in spite of all the years.

He settled next to his daughter on the bed across from Sindhu.

Sindhu smiled amicably and said pointing at the pot, "Koli is talented. Why do you say that?"

The old man looked at his daughter's face reprovingly. Koli smiled puckishly.

Finally, the old man said, "She is undoubtedly talented, but you know what? To muster any kind of skill, one must have determination and tenacity. Otherwise, talent is like an uncut diamond; it misses the edges…the glitter. Koli never fits in the snugly grasping socket of routine or regulation. She does this today and that tomorrow. I know, she leaves her unique impression in whatever she does, but that's not enough. She must hone her skill; or else your faculty stays hidden behind your unskilled mask. I failed to trap her in any discipline you know."

The aroma of a mutton dish being prepared wafted through the air, giving Koli the opportunity to change the subject, "I guess the meat is ready. I am preparing a particularly special dish for tonight."

"Do you think there could be changes in the trend of art and architecture in the coming days?" Sindhu asked the old man.

"Yes, of course! In fact, drastic changes are already setting in." The old man replied.

Sindhu remained silent, waiting to hear the veteran.

"You must have seen the old baked clay models of women holding suckling babies but today we make models of men holding babies in the lap. Is it not a change? Of course, a revolutionary change! Art comes from life and life from the social fabric. Today, men participate in the process of raising babies. And hence there is this change in style." The old man said matter-of-factly.

Sindhu replied, "I do agree. Nevertheless, my point is different. Each of our art objects is practically meant to serve some kind of religious purpose or used as a plaything for the kids. They are generally dumped after the purpose is fulfilled. The female figurines were being made to represent human fertility, and then the male variety replaced them. Only the gender of representation shifted; but it was still the representation of some important aspect of our wish list - fertility. Eventually, that tradition is also dead. Today we neither represent fertility nor religious objects, but we produce some kind of crude votive figurines to ward off the imaginary evil! Art in this land is always restricted within a narrow space carved by religious need and toys. In addition, don't you think, the designs are extremely monotonous now? The only other option for an artist is to etch some lifeless seals. That's all!"

The old man considered Sindhu's opinion and said, "You are young…and there are so many youngsters like you. You must bring changes now. We are old. We lost our ability to think beyond the habitual boundary. See, I still remember that gentleman who developed a brick of different proportion more suitable for construction work. He demonstrated the process to the council successfully. Even so, the council feared it might disturb the deep set uniformity of the empire, and decided against it after plenty of deliberations. Disparate dimensional proportions of bricks could create chaos among the masons, bricklayers and architects of different cities. Today there are principally three proportions for bricks in use. No deviation is allowed. There are pros and cons of consistency anyway. I don't deny that."

Koli listened to the discourse intently and then shook her head, "We had enough of cribbing about current affairs in art. Tell us Sindhu, how was the journey from your hometown to this place? It must have been quite an adventure!"

Sindhu reflected, "Ah! It was a hell of a journey from my town to yours. In fact, it was quite hazardous, you know. The roads were available only in certain areas and the ox-cart would not roll over the rough and uneven terrain. The oxen were scared. I had to travel almost one-third of the stretch on foot. I could not help but move on. There is nothing left on the bank of the drying river. It is almost a barren land now, parched, thirsty, sucking all the moisture from the air."

"Your father gave you the correct advice before departing. Your destiny is here, in this town. You know we have been close friends and studied together. Later he chose farming, and I chose art. It's a pleasure to get a chance to help his son. I shall try my best to find a job for you here. Tomorrow, come with me to the council; let's see what we can do." The old man said affectionately.

Koli prepared to arrange the food. "Let's have our dinner now."

She picked up the candle and said, "I shall take it for a while; do you mind sitting in dark or should I light another candle?"

Sindhu said, "No problem. Please take it." The old man nodded in concurrence.

As Koli left the room, the old man whispered, "Sindhu, come near me. I want to tell you something."

Sindhu sat close to him, and the old man spoke to him in a muffled voice. He could not raise the subject in front of his daughter. Sindhu listened in silence.

Koli entered the adjacent room. The shadowy figure outside the house was at a loss. The flickering flame of the candle cast a glow on the bushes from the window of the adjoining room. Koli placed the candle right on the frame of the window itself. He threaded through the dense foliage trying not to make any noise and finally reached the front of the window. He watched with throbbing anticipation as Koli unfastened her loose bun and let the dark expansive hair fall over her shoulder like an untamed waterfall. He could see her magnificent bosom ready to burn his desire to ashes.

As she bent to pick up the garment fallen on the ground, he tried to climb holding the edge of the window to get a complete view of Koli's exposed figure. The breathtaking sensuality drove him wild with lust. Koli was still looking at the ground scrabbling for the cloth when a sharp screech of an owl pierced the silence of the night. Startled, Koli glanced at the window. His face was planted next to the candle, and their eyes met for an instant. Koli screamed in fear and shock. In a state of bewilderment, he snuffed out the candle with a swift stroke of his hand and started running away from the house. He ran through the dense forest. The darkness swallowed him completely, leaving only the rustling sound of dry leaves crushed under his feet.

He felt a pinch of guilt, but he could not help it. He had seen this woman a few days ago when she had gone with her father to the bath-house. From that day onwards, he could never rid himself of her thoughts. He had never been driven by such raging passion in the past. He ran after wealth all his youth but was not able to manage any significant success until now. Women had never captured his fancy in the past. But the appealing charm of this woman grabbed him by the scruff of his neck. He would have proposed a marriage alliance to her but had dropped the idea because of the considerable age difference between them. He had crossed middle age, and the woman was in her early youth. Neither could he coax her with his wealth because he was not rich. Moreover, her father was a known personality in the society. He was no match for the high station of society occupied by these people.

He ran for a long time through the forest and finally arrived at an open field. He stopped, short of breath, and looked around to see if anybody had followed him. No, there was no other human figure to be seen anywhere.

He tried to relax and regain his composure. He must stop this hideous adventure. It wouldn't bring him any result, except run the risk of getting caught and being banished from the community. He must plan on a way to acquire her. If he could neither steal nor buy, he must get what he wanted, as a voluntary submission.

2

"How dare you pry into my privacy?" Koli screamed in fury. Silvery moon light swept over her tender brownish skin with willful impertinence. Girad could not find a plausible justification of what he was caught doing. Instead of conjuring up an excuse he stood there rooted in the centre of the meadow paralyzed by Koli's hypnotic sensuality.

Koli demanded with ferocity, "I am asking you. You have been watching me from the window. My father can drag you to the council, and they will throw you out of the town before you see the light of day."

The frantic chase through the forest had left her gasping for breath. She glared at him, fuming in rage. Girad hungrily drank in the view of Koli's heaving breasts that stood out proudly under the coarse fabric. Girad could not come up with a single word, but in a sudden upsurge of passion, he moved one step ahead and grabbed Koli with his strong arms. Koli shrieked in fear, but Girad choked her scream by desperately thrusting his thick lips onto Koli's.

A blinding flash of the dazzling sun barged in through a crack in his eyelids. Girad jerked his eyes wide open. It was morning! He realized that it was a dream. The day began with bitter frustration. The dream could have come to its conclusions at least! He felt like closing his eyes once more to carry on with his fantasy, but the brightness of the sun indicated that the dawn was long gone. Any further delay would spoil his chance of implementing his plan into action. He had crafted it so meticulously last night. He must get up and work towards realizing his dream.

He went to the bathing platform, and realized that, in his haste to carry out his nocturnal rendezvous, he had missed the most vital duty. The pot was dry. He could not even splash some cold water on his face, let alone bathe. He would have to go to the well. During this time, the well-room was generally crowded. Most of the people queued up for their daily ration of water. Though there were plenty of wells dug all around the town, yet there was a problem particularly in this area. One of the wells of a neighboring locality was abandoned because someone in a fit of anguish had killed himself by jumping into it. As a result, the whole population of that locality was diverted to this well-room. Girad changed his attire, and once again it occurred to him that he must try his luck in cotton trading. He had heard that there was high demand of local cloths in the market beyond the ocean. The only problem was the mode of transport. How could he get there with the commodity? He could not afford a reed-boat at the moment. He suppressed the thought temporarily and descended the stairs with the red fired-clay pot in his hand.

"Over the years this staircase has grown taller and taller!" He thought bitterly. During his childhood, the staircase was at least half of its today's length. In fact, he used to stay in a house located at a lower level. Lately, as the river had started behaving like a drunkard, the floods were too frequent. Even the original high base of the platform on which the town was built seemed to be well within the reach of the flood. To escape the flood, there was only one way, and that was to build another house on top of the previous one. Of course, the earlier floor was abandoned forever.

This resulted in a strange, tall staircase from the ground level up! The council raised the ground level by several layers of bricks, but that took time. It was weird, but the level of the platform on which the town stood now, had risen considerably over the years.

"Still this is relatively better than the old practice of entering the house through an opening in the roof. That was madness!" He thought.

He started walking though the street. He had to move fast because it was imperative that he visited the council in the morning. The plan must work. The council did not start before mid-day. Hence he would have some time to take a bath and have a quick breakfast. The barley he had stored last afternoon should still be there. After his mother had departed, it had become cumbersome to arrange for lunch, dinner and breakfast. In fact, the lonesome days in the deserted house, compounded with his miserable failure to strike any luck in trading of lapis lazuli, drove him to this unrelenting perversion. Obsession for this woman haunted his mind like a ghostly shadow all through the day. He could not get rid of it even when he was asleep.

He entered the well-room. There was a short queue of women. He sat on the round baked brick platform against the wall after putting down his pot on the ground. Again his subconscious mind dragged him to thoughts of Koli. If the plan proved to be effective, she would be in his house shortly, and in the morning, she would be one among these women. Somehow, the gorgeous demeanor of Koli did not fit in this damp mundane well-room. Girad wondered if he would ever allow her to be exposed to the sight of other men. No. Rather he would ask permission from the council for building a private well within the premise of his house. In the earlier days, that used to be the practice, but the growing population had forced the private wells to be exposed for public use. There was an edgy discussion going on among the women. Initially, he paid no heed, but quickly a few bites of words trapped his drifting mind.

"Law and order of the town has collapsed completely."

"Indeed!"

"Just imagine, a man sneaking a look at the living room of a decent household; that too in Koli's house!"

"Did she notice the face?"

"No. She could just get a quick glimpse of the eyes. The face disappeared so quickly that she could not grasp the image. It's atrocious!"

"He was watching Koli!"

"Yes, of course!"

"I tell you, it was not like this in the past. This town is deteriorating, and that's happening too fast; a ceaseless decay. How can there be control when there is no organized army?"

"Perhaps you are right. My husband tells me that there is another world beyond the ocean, and there people have organized armies, deathly arms and weapons!"

Girad felt uncomfortable but pretended to be totally impervious to the discussion. Nevertheless, he was happy that Koli had not had a proper glimpse of his face. He had been quick.

When his turn arrived, he quickly filled his pot and left the well room.

★ ★ ★

The state building was crowded with people. There was a debate going on about the many-fold impending threats from nature as well as enemies across the mountain.

Girad mingled in the crowd and ran his searching eyes through the faces. Koli's father and the other young man were supposed to be here today. They had discussed it last night when he was eavesdropping. He remembered that the young man was called Sindhu. He could not miss Sindhu, at any rate. He had an aura of abstraction around him. Though he argued with Koli and her father, he was not present with all his mind and soul. In fact, Girad initially suspected that Sindhu was in love with Koli. After watching them interact for the past ten days, he was convinced that Sindhu had nothing of the sort in mind. Sindhu was only concerned about getting a job with the council as an artist. There was no flicker of passion or desire in his eyes when he dealt with Koli.

In a way, it was rather strange to Girad. He felt that any mortal flesh with manhood would be driven with blinding passion at the very sight of Koli.

Sindhu was an exception in his view.

So, he could not miss Sindhu in this crowd.

And he did not. Suddenly he discovered that Sindhu was standing close to him with a small pouch in his hand. Girad guessed that the pouch must contain the sample crafts that Sindhu had made for the council.

Following Sindhu's eyes, Girad located Koli's father next to the platform, on which the council gathered.

The council consisted of ten grave looking people of middle age and a very old man. The ruler had a strikingly noticeable appearance and could never be missed even from a distance. A high bridged nose under a receding forehead rendered him with an expression of smugness, which was in contrast to the aura of detachment that emerged from his narrow half-closed eyes. He was indeed a rather passive character who never considered the need of muscle power but harboured an unshakable faith in the system and method. In fact, he was no different from his predecessors.

The council was seated on the baked brick platform. Two guards stood solidly behind them. The guards' role was more of messengers, than to protect them in case of any hostile situation. The council never feared for any hostility.

The Ruler rose to his feet and addressed the audience in a solemn tone. After a few general words about the social affairs, he said, "We anticipate some kind of calamity to affect our dynasty in the coming days. That may be a political turmoil or some vagary of nature. We foresee this on the basis of the astrological prediction of our head priest. Our experts also noted some disturbing behavior among the cattle. We are not new to flood or drought. We have also survived massive earthquakes. My only advice to the citizens is to be careful and keep the architecture of the town undisturbed. While building houses, please take approval of the municipality. Unplanned and irregular construction is severely upsetting the balance of our township. Also, I would like you to remain united as we had always been over past countless generations. Unity and integrity is the secret of our survival without any organized army. Traditionally, we don't waste our energy and resources to fight battles. We channel our passion into constructing a better future. We must stick to our values like before. The hunters from beyond the mountain should never get a chance to spoil our peaceful habitat; nor should an earthquake burry us under barrage of soil. We are unassailable. We shall live for an eternity."

The ruler left the podium and the head-priest took over. The stooping decrepit figure looked more like a wrinkled bag of parched skin yet his beady eyes exuded some cynic glow. He was very old. Nobody knew exactly how old he was but there were folklores that he would never die. Some mystical power kept him alive for many generations. Some said that he drank blood of some kind of animal every day that kept his lungs breathing. People claimed that he could see the future and had seen the past from the day nature was born. "I have a few words for you. The Gods are not happy with us. They are upset because we are losing our faith. Our offerings are no more pure and selfless. The Lord of Beasts, our chief deity is angry that we are not doing enough sacrifice. Please appease his hunger and we shall be saved from this impending peril lurking round the corner."

The ruler looked a bit alarmed at this statement by the priest. As soon as the priest was through with his dialogues, the ruler spoke again, "I shall clarify his words. He means we must not be selfish. We should think of the prosperity of the township as a whole at every step. That's what he meant by the word 'sacrifice'. I hope you got the right message."

After the speech was over, the council started addressing specific issues of people. People went to the dais as and when their turns were announced. There was murmur at the warning sounded by the ruler and the priest. They were not new to natural disaster yet they never knew how to cope with it. Every time, there was a flood or a drought, most of the existing settlement was wiped off. Only some supernatural help could save them from the doom. They started to analyze the statements of the ruler and the head priest threadbare.

Girad listened to everything but his mind was focused on Sindhu and Koli's father. He noticed Koli's father speak to the council, and the council exchanged a few words amongst themselves. Then one of the guards took some instructions from the old man. Koli's father pointed his finger in Sindhu's direction and explained something to the guard. The guard immediately left the platform and started trudging his way through the crowd towards Sindhu.

"The council wants to meet you. Please come." The guard announced to Sindhu, who was standing there with eager expectation. Girad guessed that Sindhu must have developed a pain in his neck by craning his head desperately for such a long time, in order to keep the members of the council in his view. He did not want to miss out even a moment of what was happening on the platform.

Sindhu quickly followed the guard, clutching the packet close to his bosom. Girad took a detailed note of the guard's face. He must not miss him later. From such distance, it was impossible to guess what was happening on the platform. The conversations submerged in the bustle of the crowd.

Girad could see that Sindhu was earnestly displaying the sample artefacts to the council. He offered a great deal of explanation and the members nodded their heads appreciatively.

Koli's father whispered something to Sindhu and he left the platform leaving behind a few samples. Koli's father stayed. He had other things to discuss with them.

Sindhu returned to the audience. "Perhaps this fellow is waiting for them to come to a decision today itself. Fool! The council is never quick!" Girad thought sarcastically.

Girad stood quietly, a little away from Sindhu. A few moments later, the guard once again came down from the platform, pursuing another errand. Girad had been waiting for such a moment.

He trudged through the crowd and intersected the guard midway. In a sudden move, he grabbed the guard's hand and passed on a bead of lapis lazuli.

The guard was puzzled. Girad gestured to the guard to follow him to the other side of the hall. The guard obeyed in a fit of confusion.

"I want to know everything that they talk about the young man who has just shown some artefacts to the council; understood? I shall see you after the council breaks for the day, and look here...I have more." Girad slightly opened his fist and offered a glittering view of more of the blue beads that he was holding in his hand. The guard understood and nodded slightly before leaving the place quickly.

Girad breathed a sigh of relief. At least his plan had started to roll! Only a faint worry bothered him that he could not spare any more original beads for the guard. The rest of the stuff in his fist was spurious.

Shortly, the old man left the platform and went to find Sindhu. Girad followed him quietly.

"There will not be any decision today. They have to discuss amongst themselves. After reviewing the samples they will get back to you after fifteen days. I shall stay here for a while now. You are free to leave," said the old man.

Sindhu nodded his head, disappointed that he would have to wait for several days for the verdict. After the old man left, he remained there, contemplating how to spend the rest of the day.

At mid-day, the member of the council retreated into their citadel, the place from where they pulled the strings of every event that occurred in the town. Girad waited near the rest room for the guards. He had been keeping a watch on Sindhu. Sindhu never left the council but watched the show on the dais with idle curiosity. In a while, Girad saw the guard approaching the corridor. As their eyes met, he indicated to Girad to follow him. They found an empty corner beside the staircase next to the grain house.

The guard spoke in a muted voice. "I am not sure if I understood correctly what you wanted. Anyway, the council asked the old man to come back for feedback after fifteen days."

The guard spoke apprehensively, unsure of the sensitivity of the information.

Girad narrowed his eyes and absorbed the information, "Good! Now tell me if the council discussed anything more about the appointment of the young man."

"Yes, they decided to appoint him as a junior seal maker."

"From when?"

"Hmm… Let me recall… I think before the next full moon."

That's fantastic. Girad smiled with satisfaction.

The guard looked at Girad's palm impatiently.

Girad handed him another bead. "I may need further help from you, but do not speak about our interaction with anyone. Even a slip of the tongue will not be tolerated. If you do, you will not be able to earn anymore. I have many more beads for you. So...are you ready for more wealth?"

The guard nodded in complicity.

"Then, bring me the identity seal of any one of the council members for a few days. I know you are responsible for them. I shall return it once my job is over. Can you do this?"

The guard considered the proposal for a while, and said, "I want five beads in advance, right now. Once I bring it, another two. It is a dangerous task."

Girad smiled scornfully. "You are a crook like me. Go, get it."

He passed five more beads to the guard. It did not matter to him because they were fake!

Shortly, the guard was back, but this time he was overly nervous. Carefully scanning for the absence of witnesses around him, he handed an identity seal to Girad.

After the break for the day was announced, the audience started to file out. Sindhu had no purpose in particular any more. He also followed the departing crowd. Suddenly in the chaotic bustle, someone brushed roughly against Sindhu. He stopped for a moment to look but could not decide upon the man who had brushed against him. The crowd shoved Sindhu from all sides and he moved towards the exit ignoring the incident.

Girad had accomplished the initial step of his plan. The following step must be carried out with great caution.

Girad came out of the citadel climbing down the long flight of stairs and landed on the baked brick lane engraved robustly between the conglomerates of houses on both sides. He must locate Sindhu now. Sindhu was unlikely to go home so early. Apparently, he seemed to be a shy person and was not much at ease with Koli. Girad recalled the previous night's conversation between Sindhu and the old man. They were discussing the process of metal casting. Sindhu was interested in creating bronze models. The old man advised him to visit a foundry that was located on the outskirts of the town. Girad knew the way very well because at one point of time he had even contemplated setting up a foundry, but the demand for metallic objects was low. So he had dropped the idea.

Sindhu was digging his fingers into a slab of meat on the burnt-clay plate in front of him.

"How are you Sindhu?" Three brawny, stern looking men towered over Sindhu. Startled, Sindhu raised his eyes, "Did you address me?"

"Yes, we did. I am Girad, an emissary from the council, and they are the special guards. Sorry to interrupt your lunch, but we have been ordered to execute a search of your body."

Sindhu rose to his feet apprehensively and blinked in confusion, "For what?"

"We shall explain but you have to come out with us for a moment so that we can make a thorough search of your body." Girad commanded.

In complete perplexity, Sindhu let himself be led out of the eating joint. In the backyard, beyond public view of the main road, they made him stand facing the wall. Impudent hands tried to seek something hidden beneath the layer of clothes.

"Here it is!" sounded a voice, triumphant at the revelation.

Sindhu turned instinctively and felt Girad's glare. Girad was holding a seal in his hand. A disdainful smile hung on his lips. "So, you stole my identity seal!" declared Girad in cold rage.

Sindhu was nervous and humiliated, "I stole your identity seal! Are you mad? What are you talking about?"

"But, this block of etched steatite emerged from your pocket. These guards are live witnesses. Any doubt?" Girad invited the support of the two guards. They shook their heads.

"Now, what should I do with you? Even before you started your career with the council you committed a crime, a heinous one. If reported, you can imagine the consequences… Can't you?" Girad spoke with a cold finality of doom.

Sindhu mumbled, "But I never stole anything! I have no clue how that arrived in my pocket."

"Every thief says that. Try something else." Girad turned to the guards and waved them to go away, "You can leave. I shall handle him." The guards left and Girad led Sindhu back to the table where he had left his unfinished lunch.

As soon as the guards left, Girad held Sindhu in a firm gaze for a long moment and said contemplatively, "Maybe, I can ignore the whole episode, provided we cut a deal. Let's carry on with the lunch. We shall discuss while eating. By the way, do you like the food? The council does not provide lunch or breakfast at the citadel. You must eat elsewhere. Actually, I have been insisting that they provide something to eat within the citadel itself. They are like a monolith you know. Every decision takes an eternity!" Girad spoke casually filling the occasional interruptions between words by munching sound. "The mutton is delicious. What do you say?"

Sindhu looked apprehensive. The face in front of him was of a complete stranger. After a long silence, Sindhu said, "How do you know my name? We have never met before! Moreover, I never stole anything!"

Girad remained busy separating a succulent piece of meat from the bone, and then suddenly stared at him with a frown, wanting to hear the question again. Sindhu repeated the question.

"Ahh… I know you well. You are new to this town. You came from the drought ridden port-town in the south east. I guess it's only few days that you are here. What else? You are trying your luck with the council as an artist. Perhaps you don't know me yet. I am a businessman and enjoy tremendous clout at the council. They take my opinion on almost everything – right from raising the platform of the town to appointing a new artist! Of course, recovering my identity seal was my duty." Girad pointed at the identity seal resting on the table next to his plate. It assured that he was a member of the inner circle.

Sindhu stared at him in confusion. He desperately tried to fit the various pieces of the puzzle.

Sindhu asked, "You mean you are a kind of adviser to the council? They take your opinion on all major decisions?"

Girad nodded his head smugly, and then suddenly changed his expression to that of grave concern. "Well, I think you must try some other trade, Sindhu. I don't think your old man can mange any luck for you. I treat him with high regard, but the council thinks he is senile now! They don't take him seriously anymore. In addition, you will now carry this stigma of a scandalous crime. Larceny is hated by the council, you know."

Sindhu was going to react instinctively when an excited bustle at the adjacent table interrupted their conversation. A few men sat there discussing about the prophecy of the head priest. They were skittish.

One of them spoke in exasperation, "The assurance of the ruler was vague. I know, every time there was a flood; the entire settlement went down several layers of mud and debris. Very few people survived. The whole thing was to be rebuilt over a mound of dead."

Another observed, "That's true. Don't you know about the drought in the port town?"

"Yes! Not a single soul survived. The town is almost a desert now," added another.

"I am sure that the Head Priest did not mince words. He never does. He means what he says." One of the men uttered the sentences cryptically.

"What do you mean?" The questions landed in chorus.

"Sacrifice!"

Silence fell heavy over the group of men seated around the table. The sudden silence was so abrupt that Sindhu and Girad realized that they had stopped talking midway.

Girad again picked up the thread of conversation in a tone to casual disdain, "So, I was suggesting that you should not pursue a career of art. You don't have it in you."

"I have not understood what you intend to mean. Are you aware that I met the council this morning with the request for a job as an artist?" Sindhu asked in bafflement.

"Yes of course I know. Though I don't understand any art, yet I know business. And the seals an artist conceives are crucial to our business process. Without my advice, they would never approve a new job." Girad said matter-of-factly.

Now Sindhu looked anxious. "So you have seen the samples I left for review."

Girad fell silent for a long moment and absently nibbled at the bone that was totally stripped off of all meat now. Then he suddenly lifted his eyes and said with finality, "Yes! I have seen, but if you ask me, I don't think they are good enough. Look I don't understand art and style, but as I just said, business is my domain and those seals will be damaging for business."

Sindhu almost jumped to his feet in anxiety. He asked earnestly, "Did you advise them against appointing me?"

Girad commanded him to remain seated. "Relax, my dear. I have not yet given my opinion to the council. They will call your old man before the next full moon, and I shall let them know my comments before that. Of course, these questions don't arise when you are convicted of theft." For a brief moment, Girad fell silent and after a brief pause of contemplation, he added, "I think, I can give you a chance, if…"

Sindhu was on his knees and pleaded desperately, "Please, believe me! I can do any kind of art-work; just any kind! I guess you prefer the conventional style. I am an expert on that. If you want to test me, give me a day, and I shall make a design for you. Please help me get this job. And I am not a thief. I have no clue how that seal landed in my pocket."

Girad asked with a cryptic smile, "I can do something for you, but what do I get in return?"

Sindhu was at a loss. He fumbled for a lucrative reward that he could offer him in exchange of his future. "Anything… just anything within my reach… but… but you may know already, though I don't understand how, that I have absolutely nothing of great fortune to call my own. Everything was destroyed during the drought. I spent the last thing of value that I had to buy a ride from there to this town. Now, you tell me what I can offer you in return. I am ready to do anything for you in exchange of your support in getting this job."

Girad considered his earnestness, "Hmm… you can do something for me, and if you do that, I shall ensure that you get the job in spite of your samples being no good. Of course, I shall also forget that you had stolen my seal."

Sindhu looked at his face expectantly.

Finally, Girad asked in a muffled voice, "What's your relation to Koli?"

Sindhu was surprised at the suddenness of the question. He remained silent for a moment and then said, "Nothing special… Just that I know her because she happens to be the daughter of my father's friend. But why do you ask? Do you know Koli as well?"

Girad murmured, "I am madly in love with her. You have to convince her to be my woman. You have three days at hand. Tell her that I am a big businessman and own a house in the town. She will never have to bother about her well being. Both father and daughter trust you. They will naturally have faith in me."

Sindhu was trying to grasp the catch of the bargain. "Does Koli know you?"

Girad laughed. "No. But I know her very well. She can gather all the knowledge about me later after we get married, anyway. Don't fret on these issues, Sindhu, just do what I say and the job is yours."

Sindhu thought for a moment and suddenly asked sharply, "Was it your face on the window last night?"

Girad did not seem to be upset with the question and calmly replied, "Yes! I have been watching her for quite some time now.

She is irresistible to me. Now, that's not your concern. You just do what I ask you to do. Of course… if you still want the job…"

Sindhu's jaws stiffened in fury. In a reflex, he raised his fist to strike Girad across the face; but Girad quickly grabbed his hand and forced it down. A demonic smile gleamed on his face. "Listen… It's just a proposal from my side so that the whole thing can be resolved without any trouble. In case you fail to convince Koli and her old father, I shall anyway force her to submit to me. You will be the only loser. Your future with the council will be sealed forever. I have good clout, you will not benefit if you double cross me. Nobody will listen to your complaints. By the way, don't talk to the old man much about my connection with the council. It's a secret matter. In case you do speak about it, I shall destroy your future. Is that clear?"

Sindhu stared at him in stunned silence.

Girad paid for his food and mopped his wet lips with the back of his hand. "We shall meet at this place three days later, approximately at this time. Okay?"

Girad left the eating joint, leaving Sindhu completely dumbfounded.

His mind raced at a furious pace. How could this happen? He needed the job desperately. That was the only way he could earn his living and perhaps realize his dream of becoming a celebrated artist someday. How could he bury the treasured fantasy of his sculptures being appraised in the faraway lands of Dilmun, Sumer and other places? But… but… Koli…?

3

"Where have you been all day? The council breaks just before lunch, but you came back so late!" Koli asked, while coiling her dense, dark hair into a loose bun at the nape of her neck.

Sindhu gaped through the window at the setting sun. The hanging branch of the deodar tree seemed to cradle the tired sun in its flailing arm. At any moment, the sun would tip out of the affectionate arm and fall into some unknown pit beyond the horizon. Sindhu kept quiet for some time and then answered unmindfully, "I went to see a foundry. They do some crafting based on the lost wax process but somehow the sizes are too small. I would like to create life-sized sculptures someday."

"Have you had lunch today?" Koli asked with concern.

At the mention of "lunch", Sindhu felt uncomfortable. He nodded silently. From the moment he had left the eating joint, his mind had turned into a cobweb of conflict. The words of the old man last night, whispered in the darkness, followed by Koli's scream from the adjacent room, and finally the mysterious meeting with the stranger offering an offensive bargain, made Sindhu almost giddy. Rationality and emotion banged against each other. He had formulated a plan at the back of his mind to coax Koli into submitting to that sleazy character. But as soon as he entered the house and faced Koli's dignified demeanor, an insufferable pang of guilt tormented his conscience with ruthless spite. It became impossible for him to even look her in the eye.

Koli watched him intently for a while and said, "Let's take a walk in the wood. Something seems to be bothering you a lot. Is it the prophecy of the priest? I heard that they predicted some disaster in the coming days. Everyone is talking about that."

Sindhu remained silent for a long moment and then said, "Yes…that's a matter of worry as well. But I don't believe much in the stars. Do you?"

Koli replied thoughtfully, "I am not sure if I should or not. You see, at vulnerable moments, one tends to believe in all kinds of supernatural aspects." Koli looked through the window and suggested, "Let's breathe some fresh air and you will feel better. Come." Sindhu followed Koli hesitantly.

"You know, after the incident last night, I feel a bit unsecure staying alone at home; even during the day. Perhaps it's just a matter of a few days and the eerie feeling will go away. But it's a fact that the town is becoming unsafe day by day. Things are collapsing fast!" Koli remarked.

Sindhu stiffened at the mention of the previous night's event. The shamelessly arrogant face of Girad with a devilish grin flashed in front of his eyes, and he let out a grunt. Koli turned her eyes quickly and looked at Sindhu with an amused smile. "Don't worry; I can take care of myself. I guess I am stronger than you. You might be very angry at the sleazy pervert, but you could have done nothing had you been able to catch him. One little blow and your frail chest would crumble into pieces." Koli burst into laughter.

Sindhu was pulling at a branch of a deodar tree, and a leaf tore off in his palm. He looked at the leaf and asked curiously, "I have been wondering for the past few days, how you got these deodar trees to grow on this river bank. They generally grow on the hills."

"You are correct; here we mostly have pipal trees. By the way, have you ever gone to see the granary located in the southern end of this town?" Koli asked.

"No, I have not".

"Well, if you see, you will find that the granary is mostly made up of wood. It was constructed many centuries ago. I have been told that a lot of deodar trees were uprooted from the hills in the north and then carried by boat to this area. Some of my forefathers brought a few and planted them here. These trees generally don't grow in this area. Do you like them?" Koli looked at Sindhu with her narrow misty eyes.

Sindhu felt her stare. He answered in brief, "Yes."

Koli was smiling mischievously. Suddenly she held Sindhu's hand and asked, "Tell me what else you like."

Sindhu remained frigid and silent. Koli lightly pressed his hand and whispered, "I know what father told you last night. He asked my opinion about it this morning, and I said…" Sindhu's grief-ridden face blocked her exuberance midway.

"And what did you say?" Sindhu prompted her to finish.

"I said I did not mind." An impish grin flashed across her face.

Sindhu slowly disengaged his hand from Koli's and stood a little apart facing her.

"I think I would not be able to do justice to this relationship Koli. I could not speak about it when your father brought up this proposal last night, but I must be open with you now, otherwise, it will be too late." Sindhu murmured in embarrassment.

Koli immediately steeled herself for an unwarranted shock and looked at him with an impassive pair of eyes.

"I still love that girl!" Sindhu said at once.

"Which girl?" Koli's voice trembled.

"We loved each other since childhood. She was my neighbor. No other soul in this world had a clue about our relationship. We kept it a secret because she was from socially lower community and my father was one of the respected personalities in society. Anyway, I would like to avoid the subject. It upsets me beyond measure. Her family was totally vanquished during the horrible drought after the river dried. She died one sweltering afternoon, under the scorching sun, begging for a drop of water. I survived the vagaries of nature, and here I am today, but I shall never forget her, Koli. I still love her! I don't think I can ever fall in love with another woman again. I will not be able to do you justice… I am sorry!"

Koli was silent for a long time and then said, "I can understand. I shall talk to my father. Actually, he has been worried lately about my future. I am grown up enough. He is old. Generally in our society, girls enter their own family life at a much younger age, but father wanted me to learn art and other things as long as I wanted, instead of pushing me into the cobweb of a household. Also, he was afraid of becoming extremely lonesome in my absence. Had my mother been alive, perhaps I would have had two babies by now. It's okay, Sindhu. Please don't be upset that you hurt me. It's okay."

They did not explore the wood anymore and walked back to the house in silence.

Brooding gloom reigned over the dry evening. Sindhu tried to hide behind the shield of darkness and Koli pretended as if nothing had happened. She busied herself in cooking in the kitchen on the upper floor. They preferred to stay away from each other's sight.

The old man returned late in the afternoon and quickly sensed the discomfiture in the house. After he settled down, Koli calmly narrated the incident with Sindhu. The old man listened and quietly left the room with a sad face. The anxiety that had haunted him like an adamant ghost these past days had appeared to have fizzled out the previous evening, but it had come back with claws bared, to gnaw at his tired soul. He was very old. If his grown-up daughter did not find a suitor before he died, it would be a disaster. Sindhu was a perfect match for her in every respect, but it seemed as though destiny had its own plans!

As evening rolled into night, the old man gathered his composure and faced his friend's son.

"Koli told me about what happened, Sindhu. It's unfortunate and I did not have any knowledge of your past misfortune. I feel sorry for you, my son." The old man said in a frail voice, barely able to hide his own distress.

"Oh! I should be sorry for not sharing the truth last night."

"I can understand. My only concern is my daughter. I must find a suitor for her now. I shall not live for eternity. Anyway, let's forget it and talk about something else. The council told me that they considered your request for a job. They will let us know their decision shortly, perhaps in three days' time. I have tried my best to convince them, but you know that I am old now, and don't enjoy as much clout as I used to during the earlier ruler's reign. Don't be too optimistic, let's see how it goes."

Sindhu quickly compared the old man's frank confession with what the stranger had told him. He was now convinced about the authenticity of the stranger's claim. Sindhu felt that the only option he was left with was to comply with the scoundrel's offensive bargain. He must be careful otherwise the entire plan would collapse like a house of cards.

Sindhu changed the subject of discussion and tried to lighten the mood. He spoke about the foundry, the lost wax process, the bronze crafts and so on.

"Oh… I forgot to mention this nice experience that I had this afternoon." Sindhu said abruptly. The old man was curious.

"I had gone for lunch to an inn. A middle-aged man with a neat beard was seated before me. Well… a beard never manages to grow on my face. Perhaps due to that reason, any face with a beard minus a mustache looks weird to me, though it seems to be fashionable nowadays. Nevertheless, due to his appearance, I could not resist the temptation to sneak a look at the man's face. Instantly it rang a bell! I knew him! He looked at me and recognized immediately. We were neighbors in my home town long back. Though he was much older than me, we used to play in the garden. It was great fun those days. He belonged to a rich business family. His father owned a good number of ships and boats. I had even traveled in their boats a couple of times. Later they shifted their base to this town. Today he runs a booming business. He had insisted that I visit his house for dinner, but I refused. He was such a lovely chap!"

"What's his name?"

"His name is Girad. In this town, he lives alone in a large house. I don't know his plans for the future. But yes, when we spoke today, I felt, in spite of all these years, he has not lost his childhood spirit; the jovial nature. Once again I realized, you know, this solitary impudent beard on the chin does not fit the image of a good person!" Sindhu started laughing loudly as if to suppress the thumping of his own heart.

The old man listened to him attentively and asked, "Why does he live alone? Isn't there a woman in the house?"

"No. I asked him, but he is not married. He is a merchant but wants a woman with a thoughtful and artistic nature! Huh! He is extremely shy and perhaps has never spoken to a woman after his mother's demise. It is hard for him to find a woman. Well, he is not very young either."

The old man pondered over what he had heard and said, "Why don't you invite him here one of these days? Introduce him to us."

Sindhu knew he had lied convincingly. He readily agreed to invite Girad for dinner. Now, he knew that his job was almost secured, at least for the time being. The chilling threat of being falsely branded as a thief by the council was also buried.

4

As they left the main street and entered the narrow gap leading to the entrance to Koli's two-storied house, Girad was suddenly awakened by a strange sensation that he was about to enjoy the hospitality of the very household into which he had been prying all these days, hiding behind the window like a creepy pervert! He tried to suppress his erotic impulses.

Sindhu had warned that he must control his passionate scrutiny if he wanted the plan to progress peacefully. Sindhu had also told him about Koli's thoughtful and learned mind. Still, the prospect of watching her from up close, and getting an opportunity to speak to her, had set his blood singing.

Girad followed Sindhu into Koli's house. After a long time, he had taken care to dress neatly. He had brushed his hair with his mother's bronze comb and pulled out the toga that had belonged to his father from under the bed. The toga was made of the finest cotton and studded with jasper and bloodstone in a trefoil design. Before stepping into Koli's house, he ensured that the toga was draped properly over the left shoulder and under the right arm. That was the style of the elite. Once more, he ran his fingers over his beard.

"So, you are Girad. Sindhu talks a lot about you. We feel like we know you already. Come, let's go to the courtyard and sit there. It's gloomy here inside the rooms." The old man welcomed them.

The old man turned right through a door and they arrived at the spacious courtyard neatly paved with baked bricks. The afternoon sun hung with its mellowed glow on the western horizon. The sky loomed over the courtyard.

The old man said pointing in the direction of the foyer, "You know, once upon a time this house used to be full of vibrancy. There, you see, that small room behind the guard-room... Yes, that used to be occupied by my mother. I had brothers too. Of course, my wife departed long back. Today we are left with only two creatures in this entire house; my daughter and me. I play hide and sick with my memories all the time. Sometimes, silence whispers in my ear. Huh! Old people are like that. Anyway, let me hear stories from youngsters such as yourselves."

Girad ran his eager eyes around the courtyard. Koli must be around somewhere and should appear any time to join their conversation.

"Sindhu must have told you in great detail about my father's migration from the portal town to this place almost a decade earlier. It's very unfortunate that my hometown turned into a wreck of haunted houses and barren lands, with shriveled trees poking into the glaring sky. Once it was a vibrant town full of promises and dreams." Girad said.

The old man nodded sadly. The conversation started off well, and they discussed about the deteriorating social and cultural fabric of their town. They complained about the destruction of the forest for the wood that was used to bake bricks. The old man became passionately angry while talking about the occasional encroachment into residential areas by the craftsmen. Time flew past.

As darkness fell, Koli descended the stairs to the left of the courtyard with a candle in her hand. From the corner of his eyes

Girad quickly noted her emergence at the bottom of the staircase, but tried to restrain his tendency to stare shamelessly at her. Koli set the candle on the floor and pulled a chair to sit next to her father.

"This is my daughter, Koli." introduced the old man.

Armed with a reason to look at the woman of his desire, Girad stared at her for a long moment and smiled heartily, "Sindhu says that you are one of those brilliant women."

"I am not sure of what you mean by that. A brilliant woman is not a rare species!"Koli snapped.

"Pardon me, but I feel that brilliance is not commonplace, in men or women." Girad said justifying his remark.

Sindhu smiled and refrained from interpolating. So far, Girad had maintained the balance of his false image. Sindhu had trained him well enough in the sort of discussions that took place at Koli's house.

The old man said, rather out of context, "Koli, our young friend says that he worships the Mother Goddess, but not the lingam; an exception in today's world. Isn't it interesting?" He knew that his daughter enjoyed such discourses.

Koli looked at him with a curious smile and asked, "That's interesting. Is there a specific reason?"

Girad remained silent for a moment and then started speaking "Look, in the hunting societies, animals were killed mainly by men, not women. Man focused on prey that sort of resembled human beings in expression. So, man could identify with their cry of terror, their vengeful anger or their paralyzing fear. This recognition of expression eased their job. But at the same time his subconscious mind wailed when he realized that he had killed his fellow creatures. Man belonging to these societies considered himself to be mean and heartless.

In contrast, they saw woman giving birth to babies. New life sprouted from a woman's existence. Man realized that he destroyed nature for the sake of survival whereas woman had the divine power to create... And I personally feel that way; hence I am a devotee of the Mother Goddess."

Sindhu spoke very little but listened attentively. Girad had turned out to be a good student.

Koli was in agreement, "In fact, the seed sinks into the soil and a new sprout emerges from the darkness of earth. Isn't this similar to childbirth? This is how things come into being - from the mother. Hence even I feel that the Mother Goddess is the Supreme Being that holds the pulse of the universe."

"But you see, the Mother Goddess is phasing into obscurity now. There is a widespread malaise in our minds, as if we are actually running away from the fact that there is a limit to how much we can take from nature. We think we can live without nature."

The old man said, "You sound quite like our Sindhu. You two must have been very close friends."

Sindhu offered an uneasy smile. To escape the discomfort, he tried to be humorous, "Well...my friend detests the lingam even more after the prophecy of the head priest. The head priest mentioned that the Lord of the beasts is upset because he is hungry!"

Girad started to laugh, "And the lord wants a sacrifice!"

Koli looked curious, "Do you think he really meant it?"

Girad considered for a moment, "I think so. He used the word literally."

The mood turned somber. The mention of sacrifice sent a chill. Sindhu thought aloud, "I am afraid that such a suggestion may damage the security of the town seriously. There are plenty of fanatics out there, I think."

"Excuse me for some time. I have some errands to run. Please carry on your discussion." The old man left the courtyard.

For a few moments, there was silence, and the candle's flame flickered in the passing breeze. Girad gazed at Koli in fascination. He was surveying every inch of her curvy profile with his ardently desirous eyes. Koli's unawareness of his lustful gaze excited him more. His eyes lingered over Koli's luxurious bosom. Suddenly Koli lifted her eyes and caught him staring. Instantly she was alert and uncomfortable.

"They are indeed beautiful!" Girad did not move his eyes but shifted his focus slightly.

Sindhu squirmed in his chair anticipating the worst. Koli was stunned, but Girad seemed impervious to her outrage. After a few moments, Girad mumbled, "I swear, I have never seen such a beautiful necklace!"

A necklace made of large blood-red carnelian beads rested proudly on Koli's chest. Girad pointed his finger at the large round beads and repeated what he had said, "They are exceedingly beautiful. I am fascinated."

Koli relaxed evidently. "Ah… they are good indeed. I bought it this morning on my way back from the temple."

Girad stretched out his hand, "Can I see that?"

Koli was a bit surprised, "You want to see this necklace? Do you want me to remove it?"

Girad nodded his head, "Yes."

Koli slipped the necklace over her head and handed it over to Girad. Girad held it casting an admiring look at the ornament.

"Such large beads; that too blood-red! Really magnificent! How much did it cost you, Koli?" Girad said with an amused chuckle.

Koli was happy that her choice was admired.

"I had a few broken gold rings and earrings. I exchanged three of them for this necklace. I think I won in the bargain. The seller was in a hurry to close the deal, and I exploited his urgency to offload the stock. Do you know about stones?"

Girad smiled mischievously. He inspected the beads closely in the wavering glow of the candle and said absently, "Yes, at one time I was in the business of gems trading. You know, these are perfect fakes made of steatite. I am astonished at the skill with which even white-etching has been done on the surface of this fake stuff! Despite the fact that its material value is dismally low, I think there is great artistic value in it. It's a rare work of art, don't you feel so?" Girad held the necklace out and showed it to Sindhu.

Koli was shocked at the revelation. "Are you sure?"

Girad replied with conviction, "Of course, definitely it's a fake. Don't you know that the fakes-market is larger than the original market? In fact, half the people never realize that they are being fooled. Anyway, looks are often deceptive, you know." Girad remarked with an ironic smile.

Koli said bitterly, "Perhaps. But it is not pleasant knowing that I have been cheated."

Girad gazed at her face, "Try loving that fake; someday you will learn to admire it more than the original. Your luck decides what you get."

Koli looked intrigued, and Sindhu was worried that Girad would commit another effrontery. But time flowed like an unbound stream, and the evening ended with a sumptuous dinner cooked by Koli. Girad cherished the invigorating flavor of the fish curry.

"After mother's death, I lead the life of a vagabond. After a long time, dinner has been a ceremony for me rather than a boring routine. Thanks! You are a lovely cook, Koli." Girad said before bidding them goodbye. The old man earnestly requested him to visit more often in the future. Girad gladly accepted and offered his assurance. Sindhu morbidly stared at the floor without any expression on his face.

5

Koli's house was unique in many ways. Unlike others, the walls were fitted with several broad windows. The old man, as well as his daughter, welcomed fresh air. They offered an open invitation to sunlight or rain. Koli's room was on the first floor, whereas her father lived in a room on the ground floor adjacent to Sindhu's room. The old man slept next to a large window, and always preferred to keep it open.

It was way past midnight. All the living souls in the large house were lost in deep slumber. The old man slept with some anxiety. The breeze rustled through the leaves of the deodar trees near the house.

Suddenly something was hurled into the room through the window. The object hit the baked-brick floor with a thud, brushing lightly against the old man's forehead. The old man woke up with a jolt, blinking to clear the darkness around him. Initially he felt that a bad dream had jolted him awake, but soon realized that something was actually lying on the floor.

He fearfully looked at the window and tentatively went to pick up the object. It was a broken fragment of some pot. Someone had tossed it into the room. Panic grabbed his mind. He turned around the broken clay fragment. A scrawl etched over the hard surface captured his frightened eyes. The old man fearfully saw the pictorial inscriptions that read, "Koli is mine. I shall take her."

He stared indecisively at the ominous clay fragment for a long moment and finally hid the object under his bed. The rest of the night, his old wrinkled eyes refused to shut for a moment and he remained wide awake until the first rays of morning sun trickled through the window. He paced up and down across the room and often glanced at the spot where he had hidden the clay fragment hoping that it would disappear on its own proving that the whole thing was a terrible nightmare. But his hopes proved wrong because it remained there all the time whenever he peeked below the bed.

He tried to forget the whole incident during the day by immersing himself into various errands. Finally as darkness fell and night arrived again, he trembled inside that the ghost of the memory might haunt him once more.

Koli noticed her father's restlessness and enquired. The old man brushed her aside by telling that everything was just fine. The old insomnia had bugged him again last night. That's why he looked haggard.

Anxiety and worry drained him beyond measure tonight and he dozed off at some point after tossing around on his bed for long hours. Suddenly there was a thud again, and the old man instantly sprang up in panic. Another fragment of clay lying on the floor immediately caught his attention. He froze on his bed. Finally he went and picked up the object. The same message of the previous night was etched on this one too. He hid the fragment under his bed. Another sleepless night ensued.

After several consecutive sleepless nights of horror, the old man fell sick and one day called Sindhu to his room. "Look there…"

Sindhu was initially hesitant but finally peeked below the bed and was shocked to find several clay fragments etched with the same offensive warning.

"Who could that be?" The old man stared at him quizzically with a faint hope that Sindhu might be able to cast some light in his darkness.

Sindhu shook his head vaguely in despair, "I can't imagine." He took a pitiful glance at the old man who looked wretched and mortally sick.

★ ★ ★

"Are you the one who has been throwing those pieces of junk every night into the house?" Sindhu demanded.

Girad brushed off Sindhu's words with a dismissive air. "So, how is your art going on? By the way, let me tell you, Koli is an amazing piece of art. I saw her in various postures. She is a seductress."

"I asked you something," Sindhu said in disgust.

"Of course, I am! Who else can claim his stake on those lovely curves?"

Sindhu glared at him. "Koli's father took ill last night because of anxiety and stress. He may be on his deathbed. Do you think you are playing a hero?"

"I am going to win Koli. How does it matter if I am a villain or a hero? I want her at any cost. In fact, the cost of life of the old laggard is nothing compared to the love of that sumptuous beauty. I don't care about his health." Girad said coldly.

"You are a sick person!" Sindhu snapped in anger.

Girad looked up with an amused chuckle "Come on! Keep your frustrations in check; I shall convey my decision to the council in a few days from now!"

Sindhu's expression changed instantly.

Girad asked, "Now tell me what the father is planning. Do I have to spend more sleepless nights in the jungle, or has he made up his mind?"

Sindhu declared impassively, "After the few visits that he has had of yours, unfortunately, the poor man is convinced that you are a genuinely good person, and your night-time pranks have made him extremely nervous about the future. Moreover, he is extremely sick now; perhaps his days are numbered… and…"

"And what?" Girad sounded impatient now.

"And… he may consult me about your suitability as a suitor for his daughter," Sindhu finished, somehow suppressing his bitterness.

Girad flashed a broad smile that appeared quite ugly to Sindhu.

"Good. I think the job is done. I know what your answer to him will be. Now, tell me how Koli feels about the development?" Girad asked eagerly.

"She is not sure, but her decision depends on her father's condition. She knows that her father will be relieved once her future is secured. Even if she has an objection, she will not speak up."

Girad laughed, "That's like a good girl. So all we need to do is fix up a date after you go back and convey my concurrence to her bed-ridden father."

Sindhu said hesitantly "Yes. That's correct. But… is it a perfect alliance? She is not like you at all. Koli is an intellectual with a creative mind. She has been groomed as a thoughtful character. On the other hand, you are a merchant who knows nothing but business deals. You will not deny that your moral fiber is also extremely weak. Koli and her father have been misled with a false impression. You have been speaking words planted by me in advance in your mouth. I shall not always be prompting you. What will happen then? Koli will discover your real identity, and then…"

Girad started laughing, "Then she will be my mine. I shall have her; perhaps I shall not get much time to speak to her for... you know what..." He was laughing hysterically, and when his laughter subsided, he said, "By the way, I would like to complete the formal ceremony before the full moon so that I can give my approval to the council for your clumsy art."

6

The old man lay prostrate on the raised platform. His delirious eyes hovered over Sindhu and Koli's nervous faces. The burden of age had proved heavy when confronted with anxieties of the recent past. Countless nights without a blink of sleep had taken their toll on his health. Threats arrived in various forms and shape denying him a moment of peace.

"I have lived my life. But I could not secure the Koli's future." His eyes rested on Sindhu's face.

Sindhu tried to utter some words of consolation, but could not form the words.

Koli averted her eyes avoiding both of them. She was equally responsible for this uncertain moment in their lives. She had always been adamant about her choice. Whenever her father suggested a possible alliance, she found a reason to reject the man. Most men had failed to stand up to her bearing. Now, the old man had every reason to be nervous thanks to the fact that they had no relatives in the town that could take care of his daughter. Almost all their relatives had fallen prey to the flood a decade ago.

"Now, I have no time at all to deliberate on this. I must take a decision. Sindhu, I leave this responsibility to you." The old man stopped to catch his failing breath.

Sindhu and Koli looked at each other nervously.

Koli tried to intervene, "But, Sindhu…"

The old man raised his trembling hand, "Let me finish." He fell silent for a long moment that stretched like an internal pause. "I am aware of Sindhu's reservations. I am talking about Girad."

He stared blankly at the wall judging his own verdict. The other two stood frozen. "He seems to be a nice person. Moreover, he is known to Sindhu. That's enough for his credentials to matter. I bestow this responsibility to you, Sindhu. Please organize my daughter's marriage to Girad. I only hope he will not reject the proposal."

"But… but father, I never…" Koli tried to mount a feeble protest. The old man was looking at her. But suddenly the light of life disappeared from his eyes. Both of them realized that he had left them.

Koli broke into tears. She felt as though the world had just collapsed around her. Her father had not only deserted her, but had also destroyed the fabric of her dreams for the future. She was now destined to live with the man she had detested at the very first glance. She wanted to scream at this twist of fate; but fate appeared to be both deaf and dumb. It always appeared in the past and never trod the same way back.

She made a calm resolve to herself. She would comply with her father's last dictate and undergo the social rituals, but would never belong to that alien soul called Girad. She had her own identity and freedom. Even if that freedom was overrun outwardly, she would remain free in her heart. No one could steal the independence of her soul.

★ ★ ★

"Do you love me?" Girad sounded curious. He was running his coarse fingers over Koli's pouting lips which seemed to have frozen. Her calm and composed firmness, even in complete submission, baffled Girad. As Girad wreathed in blistering passion and plundered the cornucopia of treasure in his disposal, Koli walked into the hellfire with an air of disaffection. Girad found this impassive endurance to be baffling but seductive. When the rage of passion was consummated for a moment, he wondered if he could actually touch this woman of desire at all, or would she forever stay beyond his reach!

So he asked again, "Do you love me?"

Koli looked at him absently. This question, when repeated, registered somewhere in her mind, and she slowly turned her attention back to Girad, "Hmm… I am yet to to think about it."

Girad smiled, ignoring his slight disappointment. "But I love you Koli."

Koli remained motionless in the same posture for some more time. When she felt assured that Girad was consumed for the night, she turned to her side away from him, and thought over the torrent of events that had taken place in the past few days. It felt strange that the most important person in her life did not exist anymore. As she closed her eyes, she felt herself being transported back to her first-floor bedroom above the courtyard. She could hear her father singing that idyllic tune from his room downstairs, which he used to sing when Koli was a little girl refusing to fall asleep in her mother's lap.

She could never come to terms with the fact that her father had died just a few days before, immediately after he had fixed her marriage with a stranger. Life still seemed to be whirling around her, as though intoxicated. She was unable to catch a glimpse of her destiny.

Once again, Girad's beefy hands grabbed hold of her earthly existence, and she prepared to submit herself to the whims of eventuality.

7

Sindhu toyed with a square steatite block in his hand, a faint smile on his face. The soft rays of the morning sun rested idle on the wooden table, which he shared with another young man. Magan watched him curiously, "You are lucky! I envy you, Sindhu. I worked for the council for such a long time, yet they never offered me the honor to design a seal to represent our land across the mountains. You started working only recently, but they bestowed the responsibility on to you!"

Sindhu heard him and said, "I could never understand one thing. When I submitted my samples to the council, they had felt that my style would be damaging to the trade. In fact, the council had consulted with some internal adviser to evaluate the worthiness of my art! And that adviser happened to be a stupid merchant and not an artist!"

Magan looked at Sindhu in puzzlement. "What do you mean? Who was that adviser? There is no such adviser to the council. It is an autonomous body. Your crafts were appreciated so much that they never had any second thoughts on whether or not to hire you. I was told that they were the epitome of excellence! In fact, the council sent a few samples to me so that I could study them."

It was now Sindhu's turn to be surprised "Are you sure?"

Magan replied assuredly, "Of course!"

Sindhu stared at him incredulously for a long moment and asked, "But, he claimed to be an adviser! Was there no one like that? Are you sure that the council did not consult any merchant?"

"No. They don't bother about consulting others. Had they been so particular about the views of everyone in the town, we would not see this silent decay in our society... But why do you ask?"

"But... but what about the seal of identity?"

"What about that?"

Sindhu explained cautiously, "Well, I met someone in the past who claimed to be a secret adviser to the council and as a proof he showed me his seal of identity. That was the same seal our council members use!"

Magan was now excited. "That means you might have actually met the thief! Who was that?"

"What do you mean? What thief? Do you mean someone stole the seal?"

Magan was clearly excited, "Yes! Sometime back, one of the seals went missing for a few days and then it was mysteriously returned to its owner. But who was it?"

Sindhu tried to evade his scrutiny and replied vaguely, "I don't remember clearly. It was some stranger who had picked up a conversation with me some time back and I lost him after that."

The day's work was over, and Sindhu left the citadel. His workspace was within the large bath that once upon a time had enjoyed the reverence of thousands of visitors every day. They felt that it was auspicious and had a mysterious charm. A dip in the great-bath could wash out the impurities of the sinful souls. But eventually over a period of time, arrogance took over the inhabitants. They no longer cared for the holiness of the great-bath. One day, the great-bath ceased to be a place for ablutions, and the huge space became a manufacturing platform for craftsmen. Still, the important offices of the council operated from there.

So, there was no secret adviser, and an identity seal had disappeared for a while. Sindhu's mind was racing furiously. Many questions were raising their ugly heads and he wanted some firm answers. He hired a bullock-cart to go to the upper-town. When he reached near Koli's house, he sat on a stone by the side of the road and waited for Girad. Girad generally came home at this time of the day. They had moved to Koli's place some time back.

"Girad!" Sindhu shouted as he saw him walking down the road towards home.

"Oh, Sindhu! What are you doing here?" Girad was taken aback.

Sindhu smiled, "I need your help. I have been assigned a special task of designing a new seal of identity for the council members. Could you show me your seal once more, the one that I had allegedly stolen?"

Girad stared at him contemplatively and said in a calculative tone, "You have access to so many seals in the citadel... why do you want to see mine?"

Sindhu tried to provide a justification, "I remember you had a very special one. I think that's given only to the secret advisors. I want to see that."

Girad looked searchingly at him for a long moment, and finally a sarcastic smile flashed across his face, "You are not looking for anything of the sort, Sindhu. Talk straight. What are you really looking for?"

Sindhu did not answer right away; his facial expression stiffened, challenging Girad's smile.

"I don't have it any more, and I have never been a secret advisor. If you don't like what I just said, I don't care. Moreover, you must have forgotten a light shove in the crowd when you were coming out of the hall on your first day at the council. I planted the seal in your pocket. Now that my purpose has been served, I don't care to put on a mask for the sake of your comfort."

"So, you stole the seal from the council just to trick me!" Sindhu said angrily.

"I *borrowed* it," Girad said indifferently.

Sindhu glared at him for some time and turned on his heel abruptly. Girad shouted after him in a sarcastic tone, "Yes, I am a crook! But I don't mind being your friend now. There is nothing else you can do for me, so I shall not fool you anymore!"

Sindhu turned and stared at Girad. "But you got something that you must return. I can't leave you before you do that. Our relationship will go on for some more time now."

Girad laughed dismissively. Sindhu started walking back to the town, and Girad approached his own home. He felt happy. He did not feel like donning his mask after his purpose had been served.

★ ★ ★

"See, I have decorated this pot. I bought the plain stuff from the potter. There was no decoration on it; it was just a red clay pot." Koli showed a pot to Girad, expecting him to acknowledge her artistic talent.

Girad was trying to feel the weight of a copper bar in his right hand, comparing it with a measuring weight in his left hand. At first he did not pay any attention to what Koli was saying. When she tried to draw his attention for the second time, he said unmindfully, "Who will buy that pot? Why do you waste your time?"

Koli looked at him in frustration and tried to explain, "I thought this would be a good idea to decorate our house with this. You don't see the difference. I have not painted a leaf or a mindless geometric shape but some other form. Look."

Girad smiled casually and said with an air of detachment, "All the same. Nobody checks the design on the surface before buying a pot. It must be able to hold some water or food. That's all. Why don't you learn to recognize gems? It would be of some commercial use. All day either you look at the sky, or count flowers on the trees, or scribble on some earthen ware. That makes no sense, Koli."

Koli looked at Girad pensively, "And you try to count your gems the whole day. I don't find that interesting at all. In fact, you had projected quite a different character when my father was alive. You are a totally different man today! There is no spirit of human sensibility available in you! Who are you?"

Girad felt tired of all the role-playing. Enough was enough! He said, "I am what you see. I am not an artist, and I hate art from the bottom of my heart. I feel it's an excuse that lazy idiots make up for not doing any constructive work. Henceforth don't try to share your idle thoughts with me. I am a busy man."

Koli listened to him in stunned silence and quietly retreated into another room.

8

"Enjoy the meal young men!" The cook himself carried a burnt-clay bowl brimming with boiling red gravy and set it on the wooden table surrounded by three men. "It was a young rabbit. You will love it."

The men did not bother to return a response. They looked worried and nervous. Quietly they started their lunch. While mixing the rice with the curry, one of them ponderingly broke the silence, "I simply can't forget the howling of the wolves from the nearby forest last night. They never cried like that in the past. It was kind of spooky."

Another man lifted his terrified eyes, "It is disturbing. I had never seen so many ants surfacing out of nowhere. I had to literally sweep the floor several times before I went to sleep last night. Then in the middle of the night I again woke up at the stinging sensation, you know. They had come back and were crawling all over my body! It was sickly."

"Outside my house, a swarm of honey-bees filled the air. Strangely, there was no honeycomb nearby. I closed the window tightly and slept. In the morning they were gone. I am sure it is not normal," said one of them with a hint of premonition.

Again there was a long pause. A strangling sense of foreboding loomed large over the dining table. Something was not right.

"Don't you think these are abnormal?"

"Are you hinting at the prophecy?"

The other two men nodded slowly.

"The insects, birds and animals come to know of such disaster much in advance. Something is going to happen." One of them muttered nervously.

"How much in advance do they sense it?"

"I don't know, maybe, a few days or so."

Again a brooding silence engulfed the table. One of them said, "Is there a way?"

None of them said anything but went on eating quietly.

"Do you remember the words of the head priest?"

The other two men started a little and raised their eyes meaningfully.

None of them uttered a word but stared at each other blankly.

Suddenly there was a firm decisive voice from the adjacent table, "Yes there is a way; and the Head Priest wants you to carry that out in strict privacy."

Three pairs of eyes froze at the sight of an old man in a white gown. The flowing white beard and unkempt bunch of dense hair hid almost every feature of his face. Only two narrow slits below his forehead exposed a pair of eyes. The voice seemed to escape through a struggling throat.

The three men watched him in edgy anticipation.

"Only sacrifice can save this land; says the prophet. But it is not for the weak hearted. And only the bold will outlive the doom. The ruler is too soft in nature. He hates sacrifice. He is a fool. Yet, the law of the land condones religious killing of living creatures. The idiots don't see the folly that the sacrifice of an entire civilization can be saved by dedicating the blood of a chosen few!"

One of the men spoke, "Who are you? How do you know what the Head Priest wants?"

"He is my master. He sent me to find out the men of guts who can organize a few sacrifices. You people seem to be bold enough. I have heard your conversation." The old man made some creepy guttural sound that appeared to be a snigger.

"Does he feel that we shall be saved if we organize a religious sacrifice?"

The old man considered the response for a moment, "Perhaps. If not the entire settlement, at least the brave hearts will survive. The lord of beasts will spare you if you appease his hunger."

The three men exchanged glances with each other furtively.

"We shall obey the Head Priest." They said almost in unison.

"Good. But keep it extremely confidential. You are aware that sacrifice is banned by the ruler. Hence, by chance if any of you turn out to be loose tongued, the only consequence would be death. The head priest would issue a secret order to execute such a person immediately."

"What should we sacrifice then?"

"Domestic animals to begin with."

The three men nodded in silence.

The old man summoned the entire residue of his strength and set himself up on his legs. Before leaving, he glanced at their unfinished food, "Have your meal. Cold rabbit is not so good. You must eat that fresh…perhaps raw, as soon as it's killed."

9

"I am really tired of my husband's absentmindedness," grumbled the woman standing next to Koli in the well room. They happened to meet almost every day in the morning as they came to fetch water. She was the wife of a teacher who taught how to weave thread from raw cotton and how to weave clothes from the cotton thread. Textile being an important trade, most young people took lessons in that. In fact, the toy models of spinning machines were a craze among the kids. The woman's household made a decent living from his teaching profession. Koli and the woman chatted every morning while waiting for their turns to fetch water from the well.

Koli smiled. "He is not a commercial person. It's natural that academic people live in their own world. I hold teachers and artists in high esteem."

The woman smirked. "Hmm… only you don't have to face his absentmindedness day in and day out! These people appear good only from a distance."

Koli started to laugh. "What happened? Why are you so upset this morning?"

The woman explained bitterly, "He went to the market yesterday to buy some grocery and found this man on the way."

"Which man?" Koli inquired.

"Another cheat in the town!"

"What did he do?"

"Of course, my husband is the most gullible character in the entire town! That man coaxed him into purchasing an ivory comb that cost fortune!" The lady spoke in exasperation.

"What's wrong with that? He bought it for you! Why are you upset? An ivory-comb is expensive, indeed! Generally, we use combs made of wood or bone."

"Yes I know it's expensive, but then it must be in good shape. He bought one that is ridden with cracks!"

"What will you do now?"

"I brought it with me. On my way back home I shall drop in at the market and locate the idiot. I must throw it back on his face."

Koli was curious, "Show me the comb."

The lady pulled out an ivory comb from the folds of her dress. Koli took it in her hands and inspected the artifact by turning it in different directions and looked at it in amazement. The cracks were indeed visible. Koli ran her fingers over the cracks with a frown on her face. The cracks glared out like ugly black lines from the creamy white piece of art. In spite of its defects, the comb did not fail to fascinate Koli's artistic instinct.

The women said, "I think this must have been a rejected piece from some export consignment. One of my neighbors is starting a voyage beyond the mountain today."

Koli replied absent mindedly, "You may be right. Elephants are not so very commonplace beyond the mountain. The primary demand is for carnelian beads and pearls."

The lady stared at her incredulously. "How do you know so much?"

Koli smiled, "I know because my husband is a merchant. He deals in various items. Gems and metals are a few of them.

I try to talk of art, and he tries to talk about trading gems and jewels! Huh! In the end, we never listen to each other. I'm not very interested in trade, and don't pay much attention to what he says. But, I know that this item is precious but not for exports for sure."

"I see. Then I must visit your place some day. I love jewels. My husband forgets that all the time! When he eventually does remember, he ends up making a mess of things!"

Both of them started laughing lightheartedly.

Koli said, "You know what, the whole business is unfair. The common people who manufacture and transport the items of trade never get to lay their hands on them for their own consumption. The items that sail everyday loaded onto the boats guided by poor sailors are meant to feed the elite of the society. The commoners are slogging to feed the fancy of the upper class of the society."

The lady looked at her with an awed expression, "Why do you say that?"

"Why? Look at what is being traded across the mountain and the ocean - various kinds of expensive jewellery, stones, exotic animals and the like. Do the common people get to use them? No. Any material for mass consumption is never traded! That's an irony."

"Oh! You think so much! I have never seen a woman like you! Why don't you come to my house one of these days? I shall learn a lot from you, and then I can shock my husband with radical comments. He always gets frustrated whenever he tries to exchange ideas with me. But then you know what? I am kind of happy with my neighbours and my own family. I think, in this life, I can concentrate on this internal world, and maybe in my next birth I shall cross the boundary and look at what is happening out there across the ocean!"

Koli laughed, "Who knows if this town will be there until that day. The head-priest already predicated the doom!"

"My husband does not believe in it; but I do. I am sure that the old man can see the future. People say that only the ruler can look into his eyes but no one else."

It was then their turn to fetch water from the well. Koli hung her bucket from the hook and released the ropes to dip the metal container into the water.

★ ★ ★

The afternoon sun was about to plunge quietly into the horizon. Koli stood on the terrace of her house, looking lingeringly at the mute redness of the sun's glow. Her own presence in the house felt like a vapid hollowness. Everything was there, intact, except her father. She often wondered if something else was amiss! Finally, she realized that it was her dreams, ambitions and aspirations. She could only see the ghosts of a beautiful past, covered with layers of dust. Often she wanted to erase the past; it chased her with too many promises. Sindhu had been a sudden flash of light that vanished in the blink of an eye. He had come and gone like a gust of wind. Koli had wanted Sindhu to stay, but somehow the strange developments had emerged like ghosts from thin air and had totally derailed her life.

She found herself trapped in a strange life that she could never have conceived even her wildest nightmares.

She had never liked Girad from the very first time that they had met. There was something unreal about him. She had always wondered about the mysterious events that had taken place soon after his first visit. The mysterious events had stopped all of a sudden, but there was no plausible explanation for why they had ceased. She tried to speak to Girad about these things, but he did not show much concern. It was not surprising to Koli because Girad was never interested in anything she spoke about.

Soon after their marriage, Girad seemed to treat Koli as an object of sheer carnal pleasure. He devoured her body with a kind of fierce passion that turned into savage brutality at times. Koli suffered the torment in silence, developing an utter aversion for Girad. Over a period of time, the mad rush of physical desire seemed to wear out too. Lately, Girad was totally indifferent to her sexual appeal. In addition, there was a yawning gap between their views of life.

They slept on the same bed, yet Girad did not seem to lust after her any more. Koli felt rather safe and comfortable. Koli detested the ravishing of her flesh, yet she missed something. Being with Girad had been like falling asleep on hard stone due to numbness. After waking up, her body hurt all over and she required more sleep!

Suddenly she was shocked as two strong arms wrapped around her from behind. It took a while for her to realize that it was Girad. He had stopped behaving like that long back, which suited Koli just fine. She hated every moment of their physical intimacy. As soon as she realized it was Girad, she turned frigid and stiff. Trying to force an artificial smile on her face she tilted her head to look at him with some curiosity.

"Do you remember something?" Girad asked mischievously.

"I remember many things. Which one are you referring to?" Koli replied with some reciprocal spirit that actually did not exist.

"At this time long ago you became mine." Girad sounded sincere.

Koli smirked but did not reply.

"Do you remember?"

"Yes." She thought ironically that it had never happened. She was free. She would always be free.

Girad did not bother to notice the subtleties in her response. He took out something from a sack and stuck it onto Koli's dense hair. Koli was surprised and in reflex, she placed her hand on the object. As she pulled it out of her hair, she realized it was a comb. An ivory comb! The comb glowed slightly under the orange rays of the afternoon sun. She stared at the comb for a long moment.

"That's my present for you on the occasion of this special day." said Girad dramatically.

Koli did not respond but remained quiet. Her curious eyes ran along the profile of the ivory artefact. It was beautiful but she could not miss the cracks glaring at her obstinately.

"Are not you happy? Don't you like it?" Girad asked, slightly intrigued at her lack of a more eloquent response.

After a brief contemplative silence, she smiled enigmatically. "This design is unique!"

Girad happy, replied, "Yes! You are correct. It's unique. There is not another piece like it."

"From where did you get it?" Koli asked gazing into his eyes.

"There was this poor woman who wanted to sell this item. I think the family must be in distress; otherwise, they would not part with such a beautiful item. I paid her its worth anyway. The vagaries of weather have rendered so many families destitute lately. The parched cotton fields bring tears to my eyes. I guess this must have been acquired by the family during their good times. I bet there isn't another piece like it."

Koli's jaws stiffened in repulsion. She knew the true story. The signs of apparent gullibility in Koli's expression had eased his anxiety in telling her a blatant lie. This vexed Koli more.

She looked contemptuously at him for a long moment then finally said, "You know, she hated you for this. Do you think I am blind? Do you think I shall miss the cracks? You could dupe that man, but how could you hope to fool me?"

Girad was startled. "What are you talking about? Which man?" He asked affecting innocence.

"The women who threw this object on your face this afternoon before you brought it to me as a special gift!" snapped Koli.

"So, you are aware of it!" Girad gave in with hapless fury.

"Yes, I know. She was cursing you! Of course, at that time I had no clue that it was you who had cheated her husband. Now I know!" Koli replied in disgust.

"No problem. Get lost! I am not madly in love with you anyway! I thought your half-cooked art mania might be satisfied with this object. I am happy that I shall be able to sell it to some other stupid chap in the market."

Girad snatched the item from her hand and rushed out of the house. Koli watched his departure and hated him more for his brazen treachery.

10

Girad stomped over the dry soil, throwing up clouds of dust around his thumping feet. Fury ravaged his mind. He cursed the obsession that had seized his mind and had prompted him to settle down with that snobbish female! The initial drive of lust had blinded him against her self-important haughtiness. But slowly the impetus of carnal desire had collapsed into a heap of livid deadness. He could not see her beauty any more. Instead, he kept running into her arrogant ego. Each of his gestures to mollify her grudges was snubbed with merciless ferocity.

She did not spare a single chance to belittle him in every aspect of life. He hated Koli more because he suffered defeat at the hands of a woman, who just a few years ago he had exploited as a mere commodity of lust, that he had secured by outwitting other contenders.

"Stay away, bloody idiot!" Girad scowled at a bullock cart. The large wooden wheels of the bullock cart almost ran over his foot. In his absentmindedness, he had not noticed the roads he had turned onto. In this part of the lower town, the houses were more congested, and the lanes were like fine grids, made of burnt or baked bricks. The lanes branching from the main street were the result of a lack of vision in town planning. They often tapered down, squeezed between the walls of the houses on both sides. Hence, even during the day, the lanes were shadowy, with towering solid walls on both sides. The carts could go only up to a certain distance, hence, the passersby had to stop and make way for the cart at some places.

The narrowing passage constricted further. Girad had an eerie feeling whenever he passed through such lanes. Today was no different. The descending dusk made the space even darker. He knew the place well. Earlier he had been a frequent visitor but had stayed away from it for some time after meeting Koli. Lately, he had resumed his visits again.

The lane was not perfectly straight but was bent at a slight angle. He could not see the end of the alley but knew that it was another proof of aimless construction. The road ended against a building wall. It brought a suffocating sensation in his chest. Yet, there was a door in the wall, and he loved going through that door. It helped him vent his trapped frustration. He pushed the door and slipped inside.

"Ah! Welcome! I was waiting for you. Let's have a few rounds. Come!" A loud welcome greeted Girad. The first that time he had met this middle-aged wealthy merchant some time back, he had been repelled. It seemed to him that the air of contentment and ease in his gestures pointed an arrogant finger at Girad's fumbling struggle. The merchant was in town for a short period to gather enough material for trade across the ocean. Also, he was selling loads of lapis lazuli, dates, dry fruits and other stuff at high prices before sailing again for another voyage.

"How is business, Ridham?" Girad floated the question casually and sat on the wooden bench across the room.

"Not bad. Well, those days are gone anyway. People have grown stingier than ever. During my last visit, I sold similar goods at much better prices. Today they haggle too much. The bloody old priest is probably right. The town is going to the dogs. It must be rebuilt afresh."

"Hmm… it's not surprising. This whimsical swing of weather has thrown the entire production of cotton and other corps into jeopardy. Last year there was a heavy flood. I guess you were not here then. So many single storeyed houses had to be abandoned, and we went up by one floor. We feared that the boundary walls might collapse. Huh! "

"Oh! I am lucky that I was not in town at that time. But somehow this flood is our lifesaver as well. In the absence of a flood, our municipality would have had to work much harder. In Ur, the two great rivers are not as whimsical as ours. They have flowed in their assigned route for decades. There is no flood. So, they had to build an elaborate canal network across the land to enable cultivation. We don't need that. Flood takes care of it! The fertile soil is everywhere thanks to the flood. By the way, what's your view this year?"

"Who knows? A drought seems to be impending," said Girad with a gesture of helpless resignation. After a moment's contemplation, he said, "See at how populous we are today in this town. Those violent conflagrations destroyed several settlements. Today, all the damn refugees are packed in the dingy bowl of this lower town."

Ridham listened but stayed silent while throwing the dice. The dice rolled and after a few happy somersaults, settled onto the chequered base conspicuously.

Girad glanced casually at the dice. "Don't you agree? You were also brought up in this town. Don't you think that the refugees are slowly taking over the spirit of the town, especially the lower town? In fact, some of the lucky buffoons are even enjoying fairly high social standing." As he said this, he thought of Sindhu and a sense of stiff repulsion embittered his mind. He did not have any reason to hate him though. Sindhu was a mere immigrant who had escaped from a charred wreck. Yet he assumed the respectful chair of an authorized seal-maker in the council. He hated all the damn refugees.

Ridham looked long at the game, and suddenly lifted his eyes with a mischievous smile, "I agree, but the refugees often make your evenings better. Just take a look into the inner room. We have some new faces there. I am sure you would love them. By the way, they are all refugees, yet with impressive curves. Hey, you lost it again!"

Girad was baffled for a moment. He lifted his eyes and peered at the doorway. A curtain hung there, partially blocking the view inside.

"There is a set of beautiful refugees waiting for us. I had spent an entire noon here in the delectable company of those lovable creatures. Try them out; you will agree with me and for sure change your opinion about refugees. Thanks to the fires at those portal towns, we have a very good collection of boobs and bums. Just go and check out the collection. I loved the one with the pouting lips and large round eyes. She looks so bloody innocent, as if the only treasure she has is her virginity. Huh!"

The curtain was swayed by a breeze and Girad got an ample view of the women inside. There was indeed a woman in the lot who exuded some kind of sensual innocence. The women were sparsely clad with a narrow swath of fabric barely covering their heavy proud breasts. The parade of swaying hips alluringly beckoned his maleness. He gaped at the female bodies for a long moment, and the forgotten wave of desire started to churn with unrelenting force within him.

"You lost again! Do you see that? I want the wager," insisted Ridham with a cryptic smile.

Girad was startled a little at the realization that he had lost the game. He flinched in regret that he always lost against Ridham, yet he played.

He opened his pouch and poured the contents onto his palm. A pale shadow of nervousness flitted across his face. He had a few semi-precious stones in the pouch. Girad counted the beads with suppressed anxiety. It amounted to exactly what he had betted. He glanced at Ridham. Ridham's penetratingly mocking eyes caught his embarrassment off guard. He flashed a stupid smile and instinctively poured all the beads onto the wooden platter placed between them. Ridham instantly snared the stones and put them in a pouch.

"What about another round before you pick up your girl?" suggested Ridham. He knew well that Girad could not help but be trapped in a vicious cycle until he lost everything. But, tonight he had nothing left with him, whereas the swaying hips of the courtesans coaxed his lust with a seductive spell. He thought for a brief moment and shook his head firmly.

The curtain wavered in the breeze, and he took another peek into the room. The woman would not submit to him out of love. There was a price. He had no gems left any more, yet the urge for an amorous night seemed irresistible.

He rose to his feet and entered the room pushing the curtain aside. He was a known face, and the owner did not ask for an advance.

After a few hours, Girad took a few long breaths of contentment and released the female body from his clutches. A profuse sense of satisfaction filled his flesh and bones. He climbed out of the bed and stood on the floor. Staring down at the woman lying coiled on the bed, still under the spell of vicious sex, he once again told himself that the price was heavy yet worth it.

While wrapping the strip of cloth around his waist he casually threw the ivory comb on the bed by her side. With her delirious eyes, she took a quick glance at the white object and forced a smile of gratitude.

11

"Look, the doomsday is round the corner. Never ignore the prophecy of the priest. He knows the future. There is only one way to escape the disaster: stones!" Girad opened the pouch to show the glittering vibrant sparkles in red, blue and orange. "The red one can save you from the strike of a lightning. The orange variety can help you to float when the flood comes. And look at this white stone. This will take you to a solid ground when the rest of the town will sink under pile of debris during earthquake."

The gullible shepherd nervously shifted his glance between his herd of cows and the stones sprawled over the table. Girad drew his attention by stepping up the anxiety of the anticipated doom, "You can't take any other precaution. Can you stop the rain from coming down on earth? Can you block the whim of the river? If it jumps over the platform, it just does. If the nomads from beyond the mountain rush in with their wild horses, what can you do? We don't even have an organized army. You can only find a way to save yourself and your family by taking recourse to astrological favour." Girad stopped for a moment to judge the reaction of the shepherd and said eagerly, "What do you think?"

The shepherd looked confused and blinked in perplexity.

After a few moments of deliberation, the shepherd decided to buy a few stones from Girad.

"Move…move!" He shouted at the herd of cows and struck a few of them lightly with the stick in his hand. The herd hurtled down the mud brick road. Suddenly the shepherd stopped with a frown. "One less!" He mumbled and counted again. Yes, one cow was missing. He called out the pet name of the cow loudly. All the cows halted in confusion. The shepherd looked around him in panic as far as he could see. The missing cow was nowhere to be seen.

The shepherd led the existing herd back home in a hurry and then left in search of the lost cow. He sent his small boy to the other part of the town for search.

Evening descended faster inside the forest. Darkness was thick and dense. The monotonous buzz of exotic insects filled the stillness of the air. A spark flashed and a few dry sticks caught fire instantly lighting up a little clearing among the trees. The old man with a white beard spelt out a long unintelligible hymn and threw some dry leaves into the fire. Instantly the entire area was filled with an aromatic grey smoke. Three young men watched him apprehensively from a distance. The unconscious body of a cow lay on the ground. Intermittently, its nostrils flared up as it breathed. After a few moments, the old man waved his hand. The three young men looked at the cow. One of them pulled out a small package hidden in his garment and started to unwrap it. The other two men watched him bit nervously as a large knife revealed itself. The sharp edge gleamed under the glow of the shimmering flame.

They exchanged glances quickly. Two of them silently gave nods of concurrence to the man wielding the knife. The old man did not turn his face but kept staring at the fire while adding more leaves to it. The knife approached the cow's throat. The moment it was about to touch the faintly pulsating skin, the old man uttered in his unearthly voice, "Stop! That's not the way."

★ ★ ★

It was well past midnight. The shepherd watched in anxiety as his teenage son rushed back home and stopped at the doorstep breathing laboriously. Beads of sweat glistened on his forehead. The eyes were wide in shock and fear.

"What happened? Did you find the cow?" demanded the shepherd.

The boy nodded nervously.

"Where is it then? Why are you scared?" The shepherd was at a loss.

"It was horrible!" said the boy in a terrified mumble.

The shepherd made him sit down and offered some water to drink. The boy drank some of it and spilled the rest.

"You know what?"

"What is it? Tell me!"

"Our cow is sleeping deep inside the forest. The cow is intact except its entrails are neatly laid outside its body next to it. Someone just sliced open its stomach and pulled out the guts and nothing more! It's dead!"

12

Sindhu set the candle on the ground against the wall and closed the windows of the room. He checked if the door was securely fastened. After being certain about the privacy, he pulled out a little pouch from under the mattress of his bed and carefully poured the contents onto the mattress laid on the ground. A large collection of carnelian and fiancé beads sparkled under the yellowish glow of the flickering flame. He picked up a few and inspected them minutely under the flame. The beads were of bright nuances and extremely beautiful. Yet, there were defects. Had each of them been perfect, it would have cost him six months' salary.

He had acquired them from the market of rejected gems and stones. The carnelian quarries were very far away from the town where the craftsmen finally made the precious jewellery.

Even the segregation of defective ones was never done at the quarry. The entire process was localized in a faraway place. The wealthy merchants reserved the secrecy of the techniques within their closed community.

In fact, there was often a rich collection of burnt-clay jewellery painted in red or black in the second grade market. Sindhu found them more stylish than the real carnelian beads or lapis lazuli jewellery. The original jewels were anyway beyond the reach of most of the citizens. He often wondered who could afford them.

When he had left his hometown, he had taken very few things with him. He had had to travel a very long distance by river as well as land. It had not been possible for him to carry much luggage. Yet, his penchant for sculpture and other form of art had compelled him to take the special cylindrical drill with him. He had received it from a neighbour long ago. The drill was not common. It was made of a specially treated rock seasoned through a complex process of heat treatment. He could use it to drill narrow holes through the long carnelian beads.

He had already dried the reddish orange beads for a long time and then heated them in shallow ovens. The heating made the beads even brighter. The degree of heating decided the colour of the beads. They could be orange, yellow or bright red.

Now they were ready to be drilled. Sindhu poured some water from a copper jug into a burnt-clay bowl. The beads would be hot shortly because of friction, and then he would dip the drill and the bead into water for a while.

It would take an eternity for him to drill so many beads, yet there was no cause to hurry. He could afford a lifetime; he had enough patience. Someday, each of these beads would be ready, and a nice thread would pass through them to form a beautiful necklace. The slight defects would not matter much. The final product would be an embodiment of his passion. That's the purpose. He knew he was thin and frail, but that was a façade of falsehood. He knew he had unwavering grit and resolve. Nothing could rock him.

After working for a long stretch of time on the beads, he gathered all of them carefully and poured them into the pouch. The pouch went back to its hidden abode under the cushion of his bed. He opened the window. A pleasant rush of wind hurtled in. The flame trembled. Sindhu placed the candle inside a cylindrical perforated jar made of fired clay. He loved this jar because the light from the flame trickled through the perforations and projected starry images onto the wall. When he did not work on any art in the evening, he put the candle inside the jar.

Another aspect of the jar made him a bit nostalgic. During the first few interactions with Koli, long ago, he had seen the unusual design on a pot that Koli had made. It was so strikingly nonconventional that it had etched a permanent impression in his mind. When he bought this jar from a scrap merchant who had collected it from a brewery, it had lost its conventional design of pipal leaves and intersecting circles. The black paint was scrubbed out because of repeated use. Sindhu himself painted it afresh. The design resembled the one that he had seen a long time ago at Koli's house.

Sindhu entered the kitchen to prepare food. He had bought some dry fish of good quality from the market. Like most people, he loved fish, yet desperately missed the exquisite taste of fresh fish. The fresh fish were available only at the faraway port towns where the ships anchored. It was too long a journey from this town. Freshly caught fish would anyway decompose on the journey back. The only option left was to eat dried fish. He loved it anyway. Tonight he had a reason to cook something special. He was waiting for a guest. A valuable guest!

The thought of the guest immediately instilled alertness in his mind. As he cooked in the cramped kitchen of his small two room quarters, his resolve to shift some day from the lower town to the upper town strengthened. The congested mesh of small barrack-like structures in the lower town was not for him. He would be living among the respected in society. He would not let the dignity of his late father down.

But an artist who crafted seals at the council could not afford such opulence. Hence, he did something beyond crafting seals for the ruler.

There was a strong demand for local artefacts in Dilmun. In the evening, he made such artefacts for the merchants. They bought those items at very good prices. Sindhu was becoming well known for his nonconventional ingenuity. The merchants placed orders for his artwork.

Ridham was one of those people who wanted him to carve some sculptures. Beyond mere business, Sindhu had reason to talk to Ridham. He wanted his friendship and confidence. There were a lot of ways in which they could be of mutual benefit to each other.

There was a knock on the door, and Sindhu opened the door with a broad welcoming smile.

The aroma of the boiling rice and freshly prepared dry fish filled the air. Ridham entered the room and took a deep breath, cherishing the fragrance of the food.

"That's too good. I hope you will not charge me for the aroma. I know your sculptures are unique and expensive. I don't understand art; but now I know why they are expensive. The buyers are greeted with this aroma!" said Ridham with an amused chuckle.

"Hmm... this is free. Moreover, the aroma comes with the dinner too! What do think of this proposition?"

"Oh! I am honoured. A petty merchant being greeted with a sumptuous dinner! Great!"

Ridham sat on the little stool.

Sindhu opened a wooden box and displayed a few sculptures. Some of them were partially complete, and a few were in finished condition.

"I think you will get a good price for this one," said Sindhu holding a little human model sculptured from jasper.

Ridham sat up excited, "Oh! This is the same lump of jasper that I had handed you the other day! I can't believe this was hidden inside that shapeless lump of stone!"

Sindhu smiled with satisfaction. His knack for realism reflected in his designs. He had tried to produce the bust of a nude male figure.

Ridham took the statue from his hand and turned it around to see the piece of art from various angles. It fascinated him.

"Do you see the uniqueness of that piece?" Sindhu asked excitedly.

"It is unique! Lovely! A splendid work-of-art my friend!" extolled Ridham.

Sindhu shook his head with pride. "Look at the arms. They are a part of the body."

Ridham tenderly ran his fingers over the arms and looked at Sindhu, puzzled. "What do you mean? Arms are always a part of the body!"

"Yes they are. But the regular practice is to attach two separate pieces as arms to the main body. In this figure, I carved out the arms from a single piece; no separate attachment! It's not common."

"I see!" realized Ridham.

Sindhu set up a display of the various other sculptures, and models that he had made for Ridham. Ridham inspected each of them one by one. He preferred the bullock cart and the boat the best.

"What about the unicorn impression on black stone?" Ridham enquired.

"Hmm… is it necessary?"

"Of course, even the humped bull."

Sindhu shook his head in despair, "Huh! I don't know why everyone wants the same thing; this boring image of the horned horse! Why don't you take a different hybrid from me? I think I would love to engrave a hybrid of a bird and an ox… or maybe, a mix of a man and a lion! How is that?"

"Oh, no! That sounds good, yet they must sell in the market. In Dilmun and Magan, the elite class displays these traditional objects at home. It's the fashion. If I offer something else, they will miss the flavour of this land. It must carry the trademark, you know." declared Ridham matter-of-factly.

Sindhu looked disappointed. "Then change the trademark."

"Come on. You don't understand business. It's another world beyond the ocean. They do have great temples and towers. Their artworks are very beautiful, but devoid of variety. They are much more conservative and adamant than we are. Everything is engraved on stone, in the true sense."

"More conventional than we are, you mean!" challenged Sindhu incredulously.

"Yes! They are. Our society offers everyone his share; maybe a little more or a little less, but not as shamelessly discriminating as they are."

"You mean the congested mesh of these cubbyholes in the lower town against the spacious luxury of the upper town is not enough discrimination?" Sindhu challenged overtly without hiding the bitterness he felt at this class difference.

Ridham smiled, "Yes my dear. It's not enough. Had you seen the other part you would have appreciated this one. There are only two classes of creatures in that country: The king and the slaves. The massive palace stands rooted to the ground with apathetic arrogance. Unlike in our land, the common men there don't enjoy free will as we do. They follow the iron rule. All the wealth is robbed and hoarded by the so called elite, and the common men lead a life of oppression. The palace is surrounded by mud-brick homes, packed closely together along the narrow, winding city streets. In fact, there is plenty of discrimination in every aspect. The rich enjoy various kinds of meat you know; cow, sheep, goat, duck, everything. The poor get to eat such stuff rarely. By the way, their drink is lovely. I am fond of it."

"Do they drink?"

"Yes. It's wonderful. They brew it fresh and serve it. Of course, it's not available for commoners. The rich enjoy it. Whenever I clinch a good deal, I go for it. It relaxes my nerves, and I feel lighter. The tired heaviness in my muscles feels soothed. I would love to share such a drink with you, but there is a problem; it should be served fresh."

"How do they make it?"

"Umm… they do it from barley. In fact, I am thinking of starting a factory to produce that drink here. The recipe is a secret, though. That's the problem."

Sindhu listened in fascination. After a long contemplative silence, he asked, "Are they technologically as good as we are?"

Ridham nodded, "Yes. They are good. In fact, with all probability, they invented wheels before us. Well, nobody knows for sure, yet they claim so. Their counting system is more systematic than ours, you know."

"Are the rulers strict?"

"Yes! The imperial rules are inscribed on stone tablets and rooted to the ground all over the empire. They believe in eye for an eye and a tooth for a tooth!"

"What does that mean?"

"Ah… well. I should rather say that the king believes in that vengeful system. It means that if you knock off one tooth of mine, and get caught, then one tooth of yours will be knocked off. Same will be done if you damage one eye of mine. You will lose one of your beloved eyes as punishment of the crime."

"Huh! You have to be careful then."

"Yes. We merchants have to very careful.

"One of our friends once fought with a local man about the price of an item he was selling. The fight grew vicious. Suddenly the local farmer attacked our man with an axe. A violent struggle ensued. In the process, accidentally, the local chap got his own fingers slashed."

"Then?"

"Oh! The rule is the rule. No one has the guts to challenge it. In the court of law, he had no escape but to lose his fingers. His fingers were slashed mercilessly in a few swift strokes in broad public view!"

Sindhu fell silent for a long moment and then rose to his feet to organize dinner.

The dinner was fabulous. Sindhu was an excellent cook. Ridham savoured every bit of it. The tantalizing stories of the faraway land entranced Sindhu's thoughts.

After a long leisurely dinner over steaming rice and dry fish, Sindhu suggested a price to Ridham; the price for all he had made for Ridham. So far he had not taken anything from Ridham in exchange of the countless artworks he had made for him.

Ridham listened in silence and after a prolonged deliberation, said, "Are you sure?"

"Yes!" said Sindhu firmly.

"It's a strange deal… I don't quite understand why you want it this way! I can pay through loads of gems and jewels. But you want…" Ridham hesitated.

"No. I told you exactly what I need as a price."

"So, now you will not take anything from me for all these beautiful artworks!"

"No. Nothing."

After another silent pause, Ridham rose to his feet and said with a perplexed smile of finality, "Okay, done! In a short while I shall come back to collect my goods. Keep them ready. Thanks for the dinner."

13

Girad handed over the little pouch carrying five small beads of gold. The man swiftly exchanged the pouch with an object wrapped in cloth. Girad took it with alacrity and slipped it into a secret pocket in his robe.

"You understand how dangerous it is, I hope," whispered the man nervously.

Girad nodded with a shrewd smile.

"You are not going to talk about the source even if you get caught, right?"

Girad nodded his head in acquiescence to the advice and after a second thought, suggested, "I don't have to talk, the seal will talk. Your name is carved at the bottom. They will anyway come for you."

"Well, anyone can duplicate that block of stone. It's just a coincidence that I had made the original." the man said in justification.

"No. The tools are not available for sale in the market. The council knows who has the tools and how many sculptors can carve that form," Girad proposed with a mischievous smile.

A paralyzing wave of fear fleeted across the sculptor's face for a moment. "You mean I am trapped!"

Girad shook his head with unruffled indifference, "No, you are not trapped. But you can be, if you ever flap your mouth about this transaction. I just want you to appreciate the mutual benefit in forgetting this exchange. Anyway, those gold beads will help you forget. If I need more, you can always earn a few more beads. Anyhow, why the hell are you bothered about these minor scruples? The priest said that the doomsday was round the corner. What is the use being concerned about safety and precautions when you are in front of death?"

The man stared blankly. Girad left, walking through the narrow alleys, between the congested blocks of houses in the lower town. The evening was thickening into a dense, dark night at a fast pace. Girad knew the way through the maze by heart. Without familiarity, it was not easy to walk with such ease in pitch darkness. Only a few windows of the adjacent houses faced any kind of road or alley. Of course, torches of wood burned at regular gaps, yet often they were put out by a sudden gust of wind. Hence, long stretches were plunged into darkness and occasionally a flickering glow shimmered on the baked brick road, trickling through some rarely open window facing the road.

Girad arrived near the exit gate of the boundary wall. Before approaching the man in charge of the gate, he stopped for a while to re-evaluate the scheme. Well, there was no going back at this stage, yet he preferred to go over the steps once more.

The bullock-cart would arrive shortly at the post carrying loads of carnelian beads, silver and ivory items along with an assortment of painted pottery and burnt-clay artefacts. After the formalities at the post would be completed, the bullock-cart would move north-west towards the river. Then the consignment would finally head for the mountain to deliver the goods at the settlement near the arid land of white snow. From there, the goods would further travel westward to settle in some faraway king's stockyard. In exchange, a load of lapis lazuli, tin, and gold would come back. There would be a good quantity of dates and dry fruits also as a tribute to the local council. Sometimes even a few tall weird looking beasts entered through the post. Camels were a better at long distance transport through barren and arid land compared to bulls.

The young man in charge of the voyage had shared his pain with Girad. They had a prolonged deliberation on this plan. In return for transporting such precious goods, he received only enough bowls of barley to last the month and a dingy shed of four walls in the lower town. This unjust compensation for his arduous and risky venture across wild rivers and arid hills demoralized him thoroughly. He did not care for the law of the land. He wanted revenge.

Hence, Girad sounded appealing to him. After a prolonged consideration, he agreed to be an accomplice in this act of robbery. When a load of goods crossed the border, the impression of a seal was taken on soft clay. It was the exit impression that was later submitted to the council to account for the goods exported. There was another complementing seal available in the faraway land. When the merchant returned, he brought along with him the impression of that seal through which the recipients of the faraway land declared that they had received the goods in good condition. This was the entry seal. The cycle was completed when the entry seal was also submitted to the council after a specified time span. Girad's plan was to hijack the goods before it crossed the border, yet not leave any trace of the hijack. He could simply sell the stuff in this town itself. Carnelian beads or golden blocks did not announce their experience of being stolen. Dry fruits did not carry stamps of approval stating if they were from an authentic source or a secret warehouse of stolen goods. So, Girad could make money from that consignment. Of course he would have to share some of it with his accomplices.

The only trouble was the man at the post, the guard. They did not know much about him. Trying to strike a nexus with him was not a safe idea. They would have to somehow overcome this hurdle by trickery.

Girad sat on a stone in the dark and watched the guard while considering various possibilities to overcome the man. Applying force was also a good option, but that would be the last resort.

Internal trade of jewellery was not very rewarding. Every passing day the margin was shrinking. People were becoming smarter about the duplicates. One could not make a killing in a few deals. Of course, there were plenty other trades, but most of them called for physical labour. Farming demanded toiling in the field. At the end, the council took away all the millets and barley. There was no way to earn much. Craft was not his trade. He hated art. The burnt-clay objects sold for a fistful of barley. Of course, building and construction were an option, and there was enough work after every monsoon. The crazy rivers left enough room for the construction workers to make some money. Yet, Girad had no experience in that field.

In addition, the councils of various settlements had such strong control that siphoning of resources was not an easy task.

The guard at the post unfastened the threads at the top of a carry bag. He slid his hand inside and surreptitiously pulled out two burnt-clay bowls from inside; one after the other. Girad kept his idle watch on his movements. The man was about to have his dinner.

As the guard let the bag slip from his fingers, it flopped around a larger container exposing the smooth green neck of the object. The flickering dimness of the flame from the candle did not offer

Girad a clear vision. Yet, the green edge at the top of the vessel drew his attention.

Squinting his eyes, he got a clearer look at the object. There was a little cap on the top of the green jar. Green colour was not common, and the smoothness was typically attributed to stone. Green-stone! Girad jumped to his feet. He got it! Green-stone came from beyond the mountain. Not a shred of green-stone was to be found in this land. Any import of green-stone through the gate was seized by the council for further trade with other parts of the world. Girad smiled venomously. How could the poor guard get hold of such a rare object? There was only one possibility. That could lead Girad and his friend through the post into the world of riches.

He waited silently for the bullock cart to arrive at the post. In the meantime, Girad fixed his alert gaze on the green cap of the object peering over the flopped bag.

After a long time, Girad sensed the wheels of the bullock-cart against the dusty uneven ground at a distance. The guard had almost finished his food and swiftly replaced the bowls inside the bag. With deft alacrity, he pulled out the green object from inside. Girad realized now that it was a nice jar made of green-stone. Gulping down a few swigs of water, he quickly replaced the cap and concealed the jar inside the bag.

"Who's there?" The guard called out peering into the darkness trying to locate the source of the sound.

Girad now rose to his feet and suddenly emerged from behind the dark shadow. The bullock-cart came to a halt in front of the gate. The rider disembarked and walked a few steps to face the guard who was still wiping the flavour of his dinner from his lips.

"I am taking those objects across the mountain in favour of the council," declared the young rider.

"Show me your seal," the guard said with indifference.

The rider fished out a steatite seal carved with a motif and briefly inscribed with the names of the objects he was carrying. He handed the seal to the guard. The guard went inside the room to check the veracity of the seal under the candle light.

"Let's begin!" whispered Girad into the ear of the young man. The young man started a little. He had not realized Girad's soundless emergence from the shadow behind him.

He offered a nervous smile and nodded.

The guard was still in the hall scrutinizing the originality of the seal. Girad and the young man walked in.

"That seal is original. But these goods will not go far from here." declared Girad in a tone of arrogant mockery.

The rugged man was startled and spun around in reflex. "What do you mean? Who are you? Get out!" blurted the guard in a nervous fit.

A cynical flash of a smile fleeted across Girad's lips. "No. We have to settle this within these walls. Listen carefully. This gentleman will cross the wall along with the bullock cart and disappear, whereas the goods will stay inside. Do you understand?" Announcing this in the form of a resolute whisper, Girad sprang to the corner of the room suddenly and caught hold of the spear resting against the wall.

The guard stood rooted to his spot, at a complete loss, glaring at the two men hijacking his post.

"Now, stamp his exit on that soft clay. You must record his exit with the goods. Quick!" Girad dictated with silent menace.

The guard posed a feeble argument hoping to dissuade them, "You are stupid. After several full moons when they will ask for the stamp of the return seal, what will happen? They will think that he has disappeared with the goods. The hunt will begin. Then what will you do?"

Girad laughed, "You will stamp that as well right now, only to bring it out after he returns."

"I shall do no such thing, for two reasons. Firstly, it is against my principle, and secondly, the return seal is different. That comes from beyond the mountain, bearing the confirmation of receipt of goods and the accompanying items!" The guard mounted a weak resistance with acute nervousness.

Girad started to laugh sneeringly, "Did you say 'principle'? Come on, how much do they pay you? Two sacks of barley and one sack of salt? Does that suffice for your livelihood? You must be living in one of those shabby holes in the lower town. You are talking about principle!"

The guard protested indignantly, "Yes, I do. I am honest and shall protect the interest of the council till my last breath. You are not going beyond the post till I am alive."

Girad held him in a firm penetrative gaze for a long moment and suddenly pointed at the bag lying in a corner. "Open that bag."

The guard was baffled, "What bag?"

"That bag in which you have you dinner," Girad said with cold firmness.

The guard looked anxious, "What is there to do with that bag? You better drop your stupid idea. I shall forget the whole affair tomorrow. If you linger on, I shall report you to the council right at the strike of dawn."

Girad swiftly picked up the bag with one hand and asked his companion to pull out the contents. In a moment, the green-stone jar was out.

The guard turned pallid.

"I guess you can't explain this, can you? I can explain. Some merchant had brought this from beyond the mountain and instead of reaching the council's treasury, it landed in your bag. Green-stone items are not for public consumption, unless granted by the authorities. Do you have the clay tablet with the stamp of approval?"

The guard looked numb.

"Well, my friend will wake up the council right now, while I stay and prevent you from escaping. What about that?" Girad suggested playfully.

The guard relented immediately, "Okay, I shall do as you want but please understand that the return seal is different."

Girad assured, "Don't bother about that. We have that with us. You simply take both the stamps. After his return, you will submit the clay stamp to the council with a dramatic report of his arrival in a dismal state with injuries. He will be robbed by the tribal thugs on the way back. Hence, he will come back empty handed with only the seal. Understand?"

"What do I get?" asked the guard now with frank bluntness.

"A share in these goods; half now and half after the cycle is over."

"But in case they find him when he is supposed to be away?"

"He will head for another town with his bullock-cart. Don't worry, he will not be around."

The guard was convinced and brought out the soft clay pellet to take the requisite stamps.

Shortly after midnight, the bulls were happy that the cart was very light. There was very little load. The lone passenger vanished into the darkness.

14

It was well past midnight. The buzz of fireflies droned in the depth of the dark forest. Suddenly a spark of light flashed and a few sticks caught fire. Yellow flare of a flickering flame came to life lighting a small clearing among the cluster of towering trees.

The stilled body of a nauseated goat lay prostrate over the grass. Three men stood silently waiting for some divine dictate. An old man with a white beard intoned an unintelligible hymn gazing into the fire. A bunch of dry leaves kept burning. Grey aromatic smoke clouded the air.

"Begin!" ordered the old man in his raspy tenor.

A massive hammer made of stone lifted up in the air and swung perilously before coming down heavily over the abdomen of the animal. The single vicious blow smashed the bones into pieces and a jet of red blood gushed out through its mouth. The entrails spilled out of the sack of bones and flesh.

"The lord is happy. We are safe for a few more days," whispered the old man.

Three men were still shaken at the violence of the act they committed. But what could they do anyway? That's the way of the ritual. Yet, they felt relaxed. The doomsday was pushed away. Nobody still had a clue as to the disappearance of the cattle.

15

The massive hall bore an air of grave solemnity. The wide timber roof seemed even more imposing and massive. The heads of the various councils gathered to formulate the future course of the empire and resolve burning issues affecting the homogeneity and coherence between the divergent settlements over the vast area.

These congregations always brought in changes as well as blocked any unwarranted emergence of power centres anywhere else. This time the meet was taking place a bit too early. Monsoon was still far away. Monsoon was critical because it was the season for international trade. All the vessels got access to the main port of the land during the rains. Torrential rain at the south-eastern port town woke up the tidal dock from its dry slumber, and the sea level also mounted. At some point, the water spilled and flowed over the dry bed of land finally to fill up the huge basin. At high tide, boats and ships sailed up the gulf and pushed on upstream, to finally berth at the dock to load the necessary goods. Once loaded and sealed, the ferries left for their destination through the same route.

From the previous night, arrangements were being made with meticulous attention given to the most minor details. A fire burned in the central kitchen midnight onwards. The empire had diverse cultural aspects. The leaders of the various councils had widely varying choices and tastes. Even their temperaments differed. Hence, the menu under preparation was wide-ranging. The best of wheat, barley, pea, mustard, rice, and lentil were piled up on the kitchen platform. Dry fish mixed with exotic spices simmered in the oven. Dressed chicken marinated in lemon juice. Tender pieces of mutton soaked in bowls of salted curd.

The head of the local council entered the hall to preside over the meet. Seating himself on the tiled platform at the head of the assemblage, he adjusted his jasper-studded robe around his body and addressed the members. He took special pride in the robe that was gifted to him by a king from beyond the ocean. This kind of attire was uncommon in this area. He wore the stone-studded silk robe only for such special occasions.

The convention started by addressing a few regular issues about intra-settlement trade. Individual councils gave information about their inventories of various raw materials and finished goods. This always happened in every convention.

As the discussions progressed, the subjects of disputes started to pop up one by one.

"We must underplay the prophecy. The citizens are pretty gullible and prone to prejudice. There are reports of a few ghastly deaths of some domestic animals in the forest. I suspect the obvious. If the mayhem of sacrifice gathers momentum, we never know where it would end," Commented the ruler. Most of the members remained silent accepting the advice grudgingly. Only a few sounded their vocal support. The general reticence about the subject posed a head-block for further discussion.

"Shall we set up a new town in the north on one of the river banks?" One of the council heads opened the subject. His settlement was the biggest supplier of burnt clay bricks in the empire.

"Of course, we must; but the rivers are rain fed. All the water from the hills is sucked by the big river in the east. If the rain ceases, the river you are talking about will run dry. What will happen then?" One member countered.

"Well, after the disappearance of the holy river due to the diversion of water, so many towns perished. So many people died. But do you think that the survivors simply vanished? No. The population of our major towns increased, and there are already small habitats at the tributary near the hills up north. If we set up our new towns formally in those new locations with all the facilities, we shall only gain in this respect. In fact they could be of use for bringing in high quality wood from the tall trees up in the hills."

"Okay, that's final. We will go ahead with this project. We will start a new town. But let's make sure that we start from scratch. Whatever is in existence now must be flattened and the new towns will be started on a blank slate," decreed the president.

"But, there is a problem. Some towns are producing bricks of different proportions, and such bricks are spreading across all the settlements. Though it's not much, yet it's destroying the uniformity like a silent undercurrent. We must bring a stop to this."

There was a murmur. The slightest sign of disintegration alarmed the councils. There was no army; there was not much muscle power to enforce the system. Hence, the web of understandings must be uniform. No deviation was welcome.

"We shall ensure regular inspection of every factory producing bricks in each settlement and in case any deviation is found, we stop sanctioning the articles of basic need to the respective owner and his family."

"But how do we do that?"

"Oh, come on! The clay tablet and the secret word must match to collect the stuff from council anyway, so what is so difficult about it?"

"Clay tablets are mass produced in every household. It takes a few minutes for them to reproduce a duplicate one."

"There is a secret code to match."

"What about bribing the issuing clerk?"

"Everything has a loophole. We have to try hard to block such deviations anyway."

"But beyond the issue of the proportion of bricks, there are more serious problems. I feel there is a slack in the control of bronze tools used in making seals."

"I agree. The tools are critical for production of soft stone seals. We can't restrict the accessibility to stones. The stones are commonplace in our land. Of course, the glazing is not easy because of the special heating required."

"You are right. Without the special tools, the craftsmanship is impossible to achieve. The flaking becomes very crude and irregular with wrong chisels."

"That's exactly so. We must guard the metal tools under close watch far beyond the reach of the common people. Any leakage will result in the duplication of soft stone seals. The seals hold together the very fabric of our dynasty."

The debate went on ceaselessly about several issues of concern. The supply of dry fruits and dates never stopped to help them keep up their energy and spirit.

As the day progressed from morning to afternoon, most of the disputes were resolved, and the conclusions were recorded as impressions on soft clay tablets.

"Hence, we are unanimous that central control is imperative to enforce control over the settlements; and we shall stop the supply of basic needs to the particular settlement that will repeatedly violate the standards."

Everyone slowly nodded in concurrence.

Finally the most important subject was broached by the president of the council. "What about our posts beyond the mountain?"

There was silence. Recently a few of the craftsmen and traders stationed at the post beyond the mountain had reported that the supply of precious goods did not reach the post regularly. Only a few consignments actually reached them. The trade was reeling on the verge of extinction due to the lack of supply from the mainland.

The records submitted by the border security had been flawless. There were impressions on seal of goods leaving, and impressions on seal confirming receipt of goods, but there was no actual exchange of goods!

After investigation, it was often discovered that the messenger was robbed by tribes on the way back.

"But how could our representatives who returned from the post recently, claim that they received nothing? They did send their confirmatory seal with the messenger. There are clay tablets with the requisite impressions."

"That's correct. This means that the seal has been duplicated!"

"What can we do now? Once duplicated, we simply cannot block the pilferage."

"Yes, we can," said the president with firm conviction.

"How?"

"We shall change the seal right away but very secretively. The new seal has to be highly unassuming."

"That's a good idea but what do you mean by unassuming?"

"Something uncommon… unexpected."

"Any idea on what the design should be?"

"Hmm… some uncommon design was once conceived but was not implemented. The man who had visualized it is dead now. He had even made a sample. But his daughter lives in the same house today. I am sure his daughter would oblige us with the same."

"What was the idea?"

"It will be a cylindrical seal instead of the flat square that we now have. You know this is the tradition in the west. We shall make a cylindrical seal with local motifs engraved onto it. It will also represent our solidarity with the empires beyond the mountain."

"Agreed, you have our support."

"Then, I shall organize one of our commissioned sculptors to get the sample seal from the daughter of the deceased and then we can outwit the crooks easily without making much noise."

The meeting ended on a contented note.

The grand dinner was organized. A delicious aroma wafted into the solemn air hanging heavy in the hall.

16

Magan sat on the platform focusing hard on the square block of soft stone. He tried to carve out the impression of a mythical image. The chisel became blunt and he once again failed to chip out the narrow and pointed tip of the horn. The flakes of discarded flint were scattered all around him.

Sindhu had not shown up this morning, as he was sick. Otherwise he could have handed the work over to Sindhu, who was a master in carving out any impossible profile on the blank glazed surface of the soft stone tablets. Magan fiddled with the stone for some time and finally landed a desperate blow with the hammer. The little tablet cracked into two pieces. In utter frustration, he slammed the hammer onto the baked brick platform and flung the chisel.

The soft sound of footsteps along the corridor made him alert. He looked at the door, squinting. Lately the surveillance at the handling of soft stone tablets had multiplied manifold. The council was determined to stop the duplication of seals, and issued a limited number of tablets before the assignment of every job. After the completion of the job, a complete account of the same was to be furnished to the store. Even the broken pieces were to be returned. In fact, the spoiled pieces were ground and used as powder to give a specific smooth texture to the seal.

With every passing moment, the footsteps grew louder. A messenger appeared at the door, "Are you Magan?"

Magan rose to his feet, "Who are you?"

"I am the messenger of the council. The ruler wants to meet you." The messenger showed him the seal inscribed with the insignia proclaiming the authenticity.

Magan welcomed him to sit on the platform and quickly removed the scattered pieces of the soft stone tablets.

The messenger refused to sit and said, "You are ordered to meet the council head. You have to come with me right away."

"Right away?"

"Yes, follow me."

Magan followed the young man.

The ruler welcomed him with his usual calm and solemn deportment. His absent, half-closed eyes made him appear to be disaffected with the world around him. The closely cropped beard and encrusted diadem atop his head induced a strange sense of wholeness in his countenance that brooked no argument. He raised his eyes and noticed Magan. Magan sat across from him and anxiously waited for him to speak.

"Do you remember our senior sculptor who passed away some years ago? We had been consulting with him on various aspects after he chose to retire from his service to the council."

"Yes I do." Replied Magan earnestly.

"He had once proposed an unusual seal design. But in those days it had no relevance. The idea was dropped. He even made a sample. It was very different and unique. I want that sample. I am sure the sample would be there at his house. Can you get it for the council? It's urgent."

"I am not very sure... After his death, perhaps his daughter lives with her husband in that house. The best man for this task is Sindhu. I can ask him to get it from there. Sindhu knew him well."

"Sindhu has not attended work today. I want the sample right away. If you know the location of the house, I request you to fetch it immediately. It can't wait till tomorrow."

Magan nodded obediently. "I shall go right now."

He headed straight for the old sculptor's house. It was not an easy assignment. The daughter did not know Magan, and neither did Magan know her. Only her beauty was well known in the town. Mere curiosity was enough of an incentive for Magan to take up the assignment. He rushed towards her home.

17

The dice rolled and finally settled on the mud brick floor etched with a crisscross pattern.

"Yes! I got it again!" Girad yelled in excitement.

Ridham stared at the cubical object in consternation for a long moment and then shook his head in bafflement, "Strange! I am losing every game today! This has never happened before. Let's go for another round."

Girad laughed, "You can play as many games as you wish my friend. You have so much wealth in your stock. Losing a little will not make you poorer in the least bit. Come on, let's begin another round. Look at my bag, its only getting heavier today! Yours is almost empty! So, what are you going to bet now?"

Ridham checked his pouch for his stock of gold beads and gems. It was almost empty. There was only one small block of jasper sitting at the bottom of the pouch. Ridham deliberated for a while looking at the alluringly red stone.

"Done, I bet this jasper."

Girad's eyes twinkled with excitement. Today he had won a bagful of gems and jewels. In fact, these days, most of his gambles paid off. Fortune offered him only happy smiles and no smirks.

"Luck is on my side lately Ridham. Be careful. Do you want to play more?"

Ridham looked at him curiously. "What other luck are you talking about?"

Girad smiled cryptically, "You see, I sold plenty of stones over past few days. These folks in the town are stupid. They have to be simply frightened of misfortune…that's all. I do that well. All sorts of threats: earthquake, flood or an attack by the foreigners… anything. The senile priest has babbled enough nonsense to scare the hell out of them. They are scouting for astrological favors!"

Ridham stared at him unmindfully considering his next move in the gamble. He casually remarked, "Yes, there are rumours of a few ghastly slaughters of cows in the forest. They say somebody is sacrificing domestic animals. Well…let us play."

The game resumed. The wager was placed on a clay-plate.

After a prolonged session, the final roll of the dice triggered another stunned shriek from Ridham, "I can't believe what is happening. I can't lose all the time!"

Girad snared the red jasper and was about to get up and leave.

"Where are you going?" demanded Ridham in desperation.

"Game is over. You have nothing left to bet now." said Girad with a glint of mockery.

Ridham gritted his teeth in frustration and muttered, "I have something. I can't put the wager on this plate now, but you will get possession of the object tonight itself, if you win. If you lose, you have to return all that you won until now."

Girad looked puzzled. Ridham was a rich man. He could have betted anything. Girad deliberated for a moment. His sixth sense told him that Ridham was desperate and about to gamble something exceptionally precious. He took a quick look at the pouch in his hand. Losing the acquired gems would not cost him a thing. He nodded in accord and set the dice in motion once more. Luck was smiling at him anyway.

"So, what are you going to put on the block?" Girad asked.

"One of my boats!" announced Ridham.

"Are you sure? That's a lot for you."

"Yes. Only, the boat is anchored on the banks of the river. It's yours if I lose."

"Done."

The game began.

The dice rolled. The game did not come to a conclusion quickly this time. For a long time, the show was inconclusive.

Conviction overwhelmed him when he threw the dice across the floor. A sense of omnipotence filled his nerves. He found himself identifying with the gods who ruled the fates of people across the mountain and beyond the ocean. The widely travelled merchants spoke about those playful gods. They said that the gods gambled and drew lots to ascertain their share of dominance. The champion enjoyed the control of the sky and rain. One struck thunderbolts when displeased, another ruled the sea. Girad found himself to be like them; an omnipotent man.

Suddenly the game came to an end, and Ridham sat with his jaws hanging in dismay; he had lost.

Girad rose to his feet. He did not want to risk his boat and gems any more. He had been too lucky this night. This was beyond his expectations. He needed to gather all his senses and plan his future. A boat could lead him to a dazzling future, much more promising than his daily run for lousy business.

"Come, let's celebrate my success! I shall offer you a dinner with the best drink of barley produced in our land! Come, get up. Maybe, I shall sponsor your night too. Just pick your girl from the lot."

18

After knocking on the wooden door thrice, Magan waited patiently as the light sound of footsteps approached the door. The door opened with a muffled creak.

Koli looked at him with a polite but quizzical expression. They had never met before. The imposing emergence of her intense womanhood at the partly opened doorway arrested his consciousness for a few moments. He stood there rooted to the spot, unblinking. But soon his rationality took over, and he said with an affable smile, "I have come from the council. I have been assigned the mission of getting some assistance from your family. The council needs your help to accomplish a purpose of high confidentiality. This is my identity." Magan showed Koli his identity seal.

In an instant, Koli knew where he came from. The typical impression belonged to the council members who partook in sculpture and seal-making. She had seen such seals many times with her father.

After a long time, the reference to the council made her happy. With a delighted smile, she gestured at Magan to come inside the house.

Magan followed her through the courtyard and was ushered into a guest room.

"Your father was a legendary artist who was the mastermind behind most of the seals that are in circulation today. But unfortunately, he is no more with us," said Magan penitently.

Koli nodded impassively, waiting for the young man to discuss the matter for which he had come.

"At some point of time during his stint with the council, he had designed a unique form of seal."

"Yes, he was extremely innovative and all the time thought of new ideas," Koli said in a fit of pleasant recollection and nostalgia.

"Undoubtedly, he was a master who is absent today but we still require his support!" Magan said with a humble smile.

"What kind of support do you expect from a dead man?" Mocked Girad, who had entered the room suddenly.

Magan looked up at the face of the man who had entered the room and felt an instant repugnance at his deliberate smugness.

"He departed indeed, but he is alive all over the dynasty through our daily lives. The seals in circulation today are mostly his brainchild." Said Magan with peevish indignation.

"Before he was born, there were no seals; is it?" Girad's voice dripped with sarcasm.

"Of course, there were! He *refined* them according to the need of our culture and commerce."

Girad sneered slightly and said, "Okay, whatever. What help do you want? Tell me. I am the man of the house."

"Her father once designed and proposed a special seal in a cylindrical shape. It was not implemented during his time because it was ahead of time and hence held no relevance at the time. During the recent conclave, it was decided that the old proposal is to be revived. Hence, we request you to give us the sample in the larger interest of the land."

Koli contemplated for a few moments and said, "I think I saw something like that when my father was alive. I will have to look for it."

Girad intervened, "Wait. Tell me the reason. Why do you need it now?"

Magan shook his head in exasperation. "Huh! Had I known the cause! The council is not obliged to feed our curiosities. I didn't ask either. My job is to carry out orders. I don't ask questions."

Girad remarked plainly, "But I don't work for the council. I am an independent merchant. I have my right to question before parting with my personal effects. After all, it happens to be the memoir of my respected relation."

A sarcastic grin crossed Koli's lips for a moment, but soon her expression was impassive once more. In a conclusive tone she declared, "I will have to look for the object anyway. I am not sure if I still have it in my possession. Please give me some time. I shall let you know."

Magan left in a huff. The husband of the lady had behaved in a hostile manner. The job would not be easy.

19

Koli rolled over her bed half asleep. The muffled rustling sound coming from the adjoining room penetrated her consciousness vaguely. In her half asleep trance, the urge to look for the source of the sound fleeted across her mind like a passing flash, but the next moment she dozed off again. A mild breeze shuffled across the room carrying the fine mist of rain. The tender and moist chill floated her drowsy soul into another world.

Slowly the fine droplets of rain gathered mass and grew bigger. Large globules of cold water came rushing down from the sky. She was splashed by a torrent of chilly raindrops. She could see the river swelling, its level rising in wild vitality. A cynical vivacity throbbed in the river's spirit. The river turned into a venomous snake, slithering over the town sweeping everything in its wake. The structures collapsed like a house of cards. She could hear the wild hilarity of the colossal waves mounting over her head. The wave crashed with diabolical passion over her body and amid the white froth she had a strange glimpse of Girad rowing away over the swaying waves.

Suddenly a loud thud woke her up. She sat up on her bed with eyes wide open.

"It's raining, I am shutting the window." Girad said. Koli saw his dark image standing near the half closed window.

She lay on her bed again, but this time she kept her eyes open for a long moment trying to wipe away the bad dream.

Girad left the room. He could not sleep now. He had got what he wanted. The cylindrical steatite object had been nothing but a piece of junk to him until yesterday, but now it was a priceless possession that held some incredible fortune for him.

He turned the object over in his hand and took a closer look at it under the faint blueness of the cloudy night. Finally, hiding it inside a little pouch, he laid down on the floor. Slumber took over his racing mind in a few moments.

Koli shook her head in frustrated resignation, "This is very strange! I have searched in all the possible places. The seal is not there!" Her face held an expression of incredulous defiance, "How can it disappear from the house! I know it was somewhere here!" she mumbled.

Magan watched her in a complete daze as she moved from one place to the other carrying out another vain attempt to execute a frantic search. He watched the fluid movement of her limbs. The pulsating rhythm of the heaviness of her languid hips and the slight sway of her luxurious bosom seized Magan's consciousness.

He drank in her appealing beauty as if in a hypnotic trance. Even the subtle dexterity in the movement of her delicate fingers, when she fiddled through the various collections of objects in search of the seal, fascinated Magan. He felt as if those fingers knew magic.

Finally, she rolled her eyes in haplessness and abruptly sat down with an introspective frown, "The object has just vanished from the house. I searched in all the possible places. I am sorry!"

The words barely penetrated Magan's head. Nevertheless, he nodded.

There was a long silence, and Koli felt a pair of eager eyes hovering over her person. She could read the onlooker's entranced mind. This was not new to her. Men's admiring gaze was a part of her life. She savoured this bit of unsolicited appraisal of her beauty; the stealthy raid of men's gaze. She concealed her revelation but felt a sense of elation.

"I am curious about the purpose of your request. Is it very confidential in nature?" asked Koli, posing innocent eagerness.

Magan startled back to awareness. "Hmm… I don't have a very clear idea, but I can guess. Frankly I should not speak about this."

"I was wondering if I could be of any help in the absence of the seal. I can recall the shape and impression of the object vaguely."

Magan considered for a while and then hesitantly said, "I guess it has something to do with the long distance trade."

"I see. Even if you don't get the sample made by my father, I may be able to help you with my ideas," suggested Koli.

"You are familiar with the seal making process, is it?" Magan raised his eyebrows in awe.

"Of course, why not! Well… I never did it myself but I have watched my father working on such objects all his life. Naturally I have a knack."

"That's admirable. My profession is seal making. I am employed by the council to work on various kinds of stone seals. In fact, my friend is known to you. In the council, our desks are next to each other."

Koli was curious, "Whom are you talking about?"

"Sindhu, I understand that he was inducted into the council by your father," said Magan with an expectation of making inroads into Koli's world through a common character. Also, by mentioning Sindhu he hoped to develop a sense of familiarity between them, dispelling the officious air that hung thick between them.

"Yes! I knew Sindhu. Do you know him well?" Koli was sincerely interested now. Sindhu seemed to have vanished into thin air. He had come into her life for a few days and then escaped silently without warning.

"Of course! Sindhu is a good friend of mine. The mission of getting this sample seal would have been assigned to him, but he was not well for the past few days. He did not report to work. So, they asked me to take up the job."

Koli pondered over something and asked, "Where does he live?"

"He lives in the lower town in a quarter allotted by the council."

Koli suddenly changed the subject of discussion and said with a tenor of finality, "Anyway, I don't have the desired sample seal. If you want, I can describe it to you from memory. In fact, if I know the purpose of the same, I may be able to recall a little more. A hazy impression of the object still lingers in my memory. You can ask the council and come back for my help... Of course, if they need it."

Magan rose to his feet and was about to leave, "Do you want me to convey a message to Sindhu?"

Conveying a message was not his intention, but coming back to Koli with an answer was tempting.

Koli replied promptly, "No."

Magan left, wondering what possible excuses he could make up that would bring him back to this house during the day, when the irate man was out selling gems and jewels.

Magan proceeded to the lower town to meet Sindhu.

The narrow lane tunnelled straight through the burnt double-storied brick buildings. Koli's house looked so cosy and comfortable, yet something was amiss. Somehow Koli did not appear to be a seasoned family-oriented woman. She appeared to be a boundless spirit yet to be trapped by the commitments of life.

Magan shook his head unconsciously to shrug off the fog of fantasy from his head. But it stuck to him adamantly. He smiled absently.

The narrow lane met the wide and populated main road. He was about to cross the road unaware of the flowing traffic. As he reached the centre of the broad pathway, a desperate and angry holler jolted him.

"Get away you idiot!"

Magan turned and saw a fully-loaded bullock-cart hurtling towards him. The man riding the cart tried desperately to stop it, but the momentum was too high for a screeching halt.

Magan was frozen in shock and stood rooted to the spot, waiting to be crushed under its solid wooden wheels. Suddenly, a powerful hand grabbed him by his shoulder and yanked him out of the way. He was dragged away at lightning speed from the bullock-cart's path.

"Don't you want the sample before you die?" asked the saviour with a broad grin.

Magan blinked a few times before he could overcome his trauma. It took a while for him to recognize the face.

"Thanks for saving me!" Magan somehow managed to spell out his gratitude. In the back of his mind, acute embarrassment stuck to him like a prickle. This was Koli's man!

"You went in search for the seal, I know. Did you get it?" Girad repeated the question sarcastically.

Magan was taken aback. He fell silent for a moment wondering if this man could read the chromatic fantasies of his mind as well. Clarity of consciousness emerged at a rapid pace. He checked himself and said deliberately, "Yes, do you know where it is?"

Girad smiled slyly, "Depends. It is a worthless piece of junk for me anyway, but for you and your council..."

Magan looked at him intently for a few moments and said, "It seems you can help us. Why are you talking in riddles?"

"Because everything has a price."

"Oh! You want to sell the sample!" said Magan derisively.

"Yes! The woman does not have it anyway. I know where it is. If I choose to destroy it, I don't lose anything, but you and your council do."

"What do you want?"

"You know, I have a boat ready to sail over long distances," Said Girad suggestively.

Magan considered the suggestion and waited patiently for Girad to continue.

Girad added, "I don't have the resources to start my venture beyond the ocean as a merchant. I hear that the council offers grants to aspiring merchants, but the process is not simple. I have no direct connection with the council."

Magan grasped Girad's agenda. "So you want the grant in exchange for the seal, right?"

Girad smiled, "You already owe me quite a lot; your pristine life was going to be crushed under the wheels of the cart. You look like a very reasonable man. You must appreciate that nothing comes for free nowadays."

Magan nodded pensively and said, "Okay, I shall come back to you. I must consult with the council. They are not very open to bargaining about matters of public interest. They may prosecute you for such an attempt, but let's see."

Girad laughed again, "No. They will prosecute you not me if you handle this in a stupid way. I shall tell them that you took the seal from me to bargain a deal in your own interest. I can even make the seal available in your custody at the time of the search! Just think how funny that would be!"

Magan laughed briefly, "It does not sound very smart, you know. Plan something else. Anyway, I shall try to see what can be done about the grant. By the way, where shall we meet next, at your home?"

Girad shook his head, "No. That stupid woman would not like the fact that I have stolen her junk. Let's meet here tomorrow right after sundown."

Magan agreed and left for home.

The following morning, Sindhu was trying to focus on work but somehow could not. Magan's unusually euphoric mood distracted him all the time.

"You have almost become a singer, my friend," Sindhu teased Magan. Magan cast an oblique glance at him and started singing louder. Sindhu halted in amusement and stared at him with a curious chuckle. "And, the songs are not religious anymore!"

Magan stopped midway and looked at him with a twinkle in his eyes, "Then? What are they?"

"Romantic!"

"I just developed the knack for romantic tunes, you know!"

"From last afternoon, it appears to be." Sindhu remarked with a hint of mischief.

Magan grinned.

With an expression of mock thoughtfulness, Sindhu said, "I feel that you have been infected by romantic tunes after your visit to the owner of the seal last evening."

The stupid smile remained fixed on Magan's face. He did not reply and only smiled.

Sindhu left the work-bench to have a late lunch. As he was about to disappear around the corridor corner, Magan shouted, "Hey! Do whatever you want, but please let me coordinate with the lady, you understand?"

Sindhu did not respond. He understood Magan's situation pretty well. The poor young man had fallen for the well-endowed beauty. It was not unexpected. He shrugged the thought out of his mind. There were other important things to handle right now.

20

During this hour the council broke for the day, and the ruler retired to his chamber. Only a few people occasionally received an invitation to visit him during this hour of leisure in case if any crucial strategic issue was to be discussed.

The ruler admired the young man. Whenever he felt like sharing his thoughts, he invited the young man to his chamber. He enjoyed the discussions with such thoughtful fresh mind.

As the young man stood at the entrance, the ruler took a quick look around and bid him enter and sit on the upraised platform against the wall. The hard and rough burnt brick surface was covered with a cushion stuffed with the softest cotton that the land could offer.

The young man sat there silently and watched the ruler, who was engrossed in doing something that appeared to be strange.

He tried to grasp the purpose of the strange exercise. Though it looked funny, yet he knew there was some sense in what the ruler was doing. The ruler was known to be an extremely scholarly man.

Marking a point on the floor, the ruler rolled a stick longitudinally, starting from the marked point.

After rolling the stick for a long time, the ruler stopped at some distance and set another mark on the floor. Then he brought in a few supporting objects to stand the stick upright on the floor.

"Do you know what this means?" he raised his usual delirious half-closed eyes without arching his eyebrows.

The young man was perplexed and amused internally but posed an indifferent expression. "No."

"If you position your eyes in line with the line of measurement from the starting mark, the height of the stick would be identical to the diameter of the moon as you see it from the earth," said the ruler nonchalantly.

The young man felt curious and did as indicated. The stick indeed seemed to be of the same size as the moon! He felt excited and involuntarily asked, "How did you know?"

The ruler smiled faintly, "It's an old wisdom passed on from generation to generation. Had you been familiar with the town planning activities, you would have known that a certain number reflects everywhere. That number is hundred and eight."

"Hundred and eight!"

"Yes. Most of the measurements linked with the dimension of the towns revolve around that number. Few are aware that the number has a divine significance. I placed the stick a hundred and eight times of its length away from my point of observation. Its height is the same as that of the diameter of the moon as we see in the sky."

"But you say that this divine significance is not known to most of the people."

"Yes, that's right. But the number is crucial to establish consistency in our town planning and architecture over the entire spread of the civilization, over an uncountable number of generations."

The young man pondered awhile and said with calculative caution, "But, what happens if such a secret is lost with the select few of the society? It is not public knowledge."

"What do you mean?"

"What if the divine significance is forgotten by mankind tomorrow?"

There was silence. The ruler considered the possibility.

The young man said, "Maybe someday some town planner will wonder at the uncanny fancy of his predecessors for the strange number and will finally discard the same. There would be no divine reason afterwards to stick to any specific number for town planning anymore. Every town will grow according to its own fancy. The underlying discipline of consistency will be totally compromised. The far reaching result could be a complete collapse of the civilization, arising out of conflicts stemming from diversity among the towns."

The ruler weighed what he heard and looked pensive. After a long moment's silence, he changed the subject, "So, did you get the sample seal?"

"No. The situation is complex."

"Describe."

"The lady's husband seems to have removed the object from her possession surreptitiously and is now bargaining with Magan for the same. The lady has no clue of its whereabouts."

"We can bring him here and employ other means to get it from him."

"We can, but I feel we can do much more. If you allow I would like to make a suggestion."

"Go on."

"We can negotiate a deal."

"A deal! I shall tell you a little more about this situation. This man who happens to be married to the late master's daughter has been under our constant watch lately. He is suspected to have committed several crimes. He kept a few duplicate seals in his possession and also possibly organized several robberies at the border. He is apparently the mastermind behind most of these misdeeds. And he is not alone. He has a set of followers spread across the population, destroying the integrity of the land. Why should we cut a deal with such a crook?"

"Exactly! I once more urge you to kindly visualize the consequence of losing the divine significance of hundred and eight forever."

The ruler stared at him thoughtfully and asked him to explain what he meant.

The young man accepted the ruler's indulgence and said, "It's the same risk I fear. The very idea behind the seal will be at stake if the seal is stolen during the next voyage. I have been told that the seal's design is unique. Such a rare mix of symbols and shapes between the two cultures will not be conceived easily again. In fact, I hear it was supposedly cylindrical in shape. Unless we get to study the same, we shall never know how it was made from stone. In a nutshell, we must ensure that the seal gets a safe passage."

"And how is that going to be achieved if we negotiate with an alleged criminal?"

"By holding him responsible for the safety of the article."

"You mean he will be the seal's guardian," said the ruler contemplatively.

"Yes!"

"And how is that?"

"We summon him here in front of the council and announce that his misdeeds are known to the authorities. His allies are known as well. He can be convicted anytime the authority wished."

"Then?"

"Then we offer him an option; the option he is bargaining for. He himself will carry the next consignment to the settlement across the mountains and to the faraway land. He will be the guardian of the seal. If anything goes wrong, he will be held responsible and punished in the most terrible manner. That way, we shall ensure the safety of the seal from other miscreants as well. He knows best how to thwart others in his line of business."

"You mean he will hand over the new cylindrical seal to our settlements in faraway lands."

"Yes. We can even make it foolproof by sending another emissary from here after some time, and persuade him to stay there for a longer period of time, offering him more subsidies on the pretext of additional trade. The impression of the return seal can be brought back by this other person, who will be our confidante. Girad is a greedy chap. If he earns well, he might even end up settling there itself. In that case, we shall get rid of an entire chain of thieves and also ensure the security of our seal forever."

The ruler absorbed the idea in deep meditative silence and after a long pause nodded in acceptance. A glad appreciative smile appeared on his face.

The idea was implemented.

Just before the young man left his chamber, the ruler said with an indulging smile, "I shall think about preserving secrets too. I like your thoughts."

21

The ruler knocked lightly on the wooden door and waited for a response. The door was ajar. For a long moment there was silence. Then a voice sounded, "Come in ruler." It was no surprise. The head priest always knew who was at his doorstep. He never had to actually see. In any case, his eyesight had grown extremely weak over the years.

The ruler pushed the door open and entered. The spacious room had no window but just a few narrow openings on the ground that did the ventilation. Two candles burnt all the time lighting up the baked brick walls and floor faintly. Various kinds of weird effigies rested against the wall. Aromatic leaves and dry wood kept burning spewing grey smoke. At first, the ruler was choked at the intensity of the smoke but then managed to remain steady. He rarely paid a visit to this chamber. The unearthly ambience inside these four walls made him uncomfortable.

"Tell me what you want," said the Head-priest without looking at the ruler.

"There are rumours!" The Ruler came straight to the point.

"What rumour?"

"Some people are killing harmless domestic animals…that too in a ghastly manner."

"We are meat-eaters. How can we get meat if animals are not slaughtered?"

"You know what I mean. These are not meat-eaters."

"Elaborate. I don't like riddles." The head priest sounded irked.

"Some people are making sacrifices, it seems; and they are following the ancient brutal rites."

"What is wrong? The doom is coming. The only way to ward off such a disaster, if at all possible, is through intensive sacrifice. Anyway, we kill enough cows and goats for lunch and dinners. This will save countless human lives at the cost of a few mindless beasts."

"I had banned sacrifice in this settlement."

"I don't care."

"Hmm…that means you have been organizing those mean clandestine activities!"

The head priest raised his eyes for the first time. A flicker of anger crossed his wrinkled countenance. After a brief pause, he said, "No. I have not ordered any sacrifice, but I don't condone it either. And I don't share your views. You will lead this town to cataclysm."

21

In a few days, Girad appeared in front of the council.

"I want to go to Dilmun. I hear that there is a heavy demand for our articles among the aristocrats of Dilmun."

"Well, we are planning to send an expedition to Dilmun, but how will you travel such a long distance?"

Girad remained silent.

"Even if we offer you some space in our sea-faring vessel that leaves the port soon after the monsoon wind's arrival, you have to anyway reach the port, which as you know is not just next door! You need a boat to sail through the river, and a few porters to tow it along the coastline. The consignments we send to Dilmun are much more than we send to our settlements beyond the mountain. Moreover, you will have your own goods to sell. Bullock-carts will also not work."

"I already have a boat. I just need some space in the vessel; also, some porters to help me trace the coastline. I shall manage the rest."

"So, you already have a boat! Then we can sanction your voyage to Dilmun. Anyway, once more we would like to remind you that any mishap with the seal or the consignment will result in severe consequences."

Girad nodded wearily. He had to take up the challenge; there was no other option.

During the night of the subsequent full moon, he was to leave the town with his large consignment. Fortune awaited him beyond the ocean, he knew it for sure!

BOOK II

22

The boat carrying Girad and his goods sailed along the river. The image of the sailor and his boat slowly faded on the horizon. He must reach the coast in time to board the large seafaring vessel; the real ship that would carry him across the ocean to the land of Dilmun. His dream of becoming a real merchant would come true. He would come back rich.

There was a large gathering at the bank to see him off. Both Sindhu and Magan were deputed to ensure a smooth send off with the new seal. The formalities were a bit more thorough this time around, mainly because of Girad's reputation of poor integrity and also because the guards at the various check points were not familiar with the new seal yet. Koli had also come. She stood silently, watching the disappearing boat.

The timing was crucial because the direction of the wind did not wait for a missing passenger or a missing load of jewels and garments. The monsoon wind was punctual but indifferent. It did not care for human concern. Hence, the vessel from the southern coastal port followed the wind religiously. In addition, the dock dried up after the monsoon. The ships could sail only after the rains flooded the shallow channels and filled the basin. Anyway, Girad left well in advance to secure his space on the deck. In fact, he was a special guest because of the seal.

All three of them stared at the horizon for a long moment even after the boat had disappeared. Magan and Sindhu stood a little apart from Koli.

Koli and Sindhu had not met each other for a long time. Time seemed to have separated them reasonably well. However, they had not spoken to each other on the river bank. The vanishing boat acted as a pretext for avoiding eye contact.

Magan felt edgy. He had managed to have a surreptitious exchange with Girad before he had departed. Magan had bought something; a necklace made of carnelian beads. It was expensive because Magan had wanted an original version. Girad tried to shove three different spurious varieties one after the other at him, but Magan could not be fooled. He had spent half his life among stones. Finally Girad gave up and produced an original. Magan held the treasure dearly within his palm wrapped in a soft cloth. He had his plans. He was tempted to break the silence and suggest accompanying Koli to her house, but the silence was too heavy.

Darkness was descending. A cold and moist breeze swept over the bank. Suddenly Koli looked at Sindhu and said, "You have to take me home. It's not safe in the evening. We are outside the town limits."

Sindhu nodded and after staring blankly at the river for a moment, turned to begin his return journey. Magan was at a loss. His plans were foiled, because Koli herself had asked Sindhu to walk her back home. He would have to take a different route to the lower town. He did not think that tagging along with them would be a good idea.

Just before they started out, Magan whispered into Sindhu's ear, "Just try to understand what she thinks about me."

Sindhu frowned at him in mock irritation, "You idiot! I am not a mediator. Take care of your concerns yourself."

Magan held his hand and spoke earnestly, "Please, I shall do my part. You are my good friend; help me. Tell her that I am a genius."

Sindhu teased, "Okay, I can bluff about that, but how can I convince her that you are handsome? You look like a buffoon! What about that?"

Magan smiled, "That is my challenge. Anyway, I ordered a new set of clothes, and also I am going to change my hairstyle. You will see then... But for now, you have to project me as a brilliant young man."

"Man or boy?"

"Come on! Now go!" Magan started to laugh.

"What is that in your hand?" Sindhu noticed the object he was clutching.

Magan looked slightly uneasy and evaded the answer, "I shall tell you later. Now it's getting dark. I think you should go."

"Are you coming?" Koli addressed Sindhu.

They bid Magan goodbye and turned back for town.

Sindhu broke the brief silence after a few moments, "It's a long journey but rewarding."

Koli nodded in agreement but said nothing.

Sindhu added, "It's very challenging, almost an adventure. I would have loved to go on such a trip to a faraway land, but..."

Koli looked at him, "You never wanted to be a merchant, did you?"

"No, I did not, but always appreciated the good part of being in that trade." Sindhu admitted.

"A merchant takes little more than what he gives. Can you do that?"

"Who knows? I never tried. Maybe I can do it better than a merchant. By the way, don't worry; there will be many people from our land around Girad. He will be able to speak in his mother tongue even in those places. Plenty of craftsmen from here have settled there forever."

Koli changed the subject abruptly, "Why did you never come and meet us for so long?"

"I was very busy with this seal affair. The council is loading us with too much work. We are only a few artists on the job; we have no breathing space."

They fell silent. There was a lot to talk about, but somehow the conversation halted. They hurried to reach the town before it got very dark. Inside the town, there would be fires burning by the sides of the streets, but beyond the town limit there was no light.

Suddenly Sindhu said, "You must be sad."

Koli looked at him with an inquisitive frown, "Why should I be?"

"Girad shall be away for a long time…"

Koli did not reply. After a long silence, she asked, "Have you found a girl to marry?"

Sindhu started laughing. "The council does not spare me time enough to find a girl. I always end up finding seals around me! Do you know any?"

Koli smiled in response. "I shall keep my eyes open. You seem to have no social life at all. Why don't you come to my house sometimes? We had so many common subjects to talk about."

Sindhu nodded, "I shall. By the way, we are inside the town now. Do you think you can walk the rest of the way on your own? I need to take a different route from here as I live in the lower town. In fact, you can get a cart from here."

Sindhu went on his way and Koli climbed into a cart.

23

Koli turned the corner at the end of the lane and arrived at her house. Several sacks of barley and vegetables made it difficult for her to open the door latch. As she was adjusting the sacks between her hands, someone called out, "Can I help you? Give me those sacks. Set your hand free and open the door."

Koli was startled and turned around. It was Magan.

"You! What are you doing here?" Koli was curious.

"I have been waiting for you. I just arrived... I mean I was passing by and..." Magan fumbled in embarrassment.

Koli smiled, "That's very nice of you. Please come inside. You mean you were passing by and happened to see me here, is it?"

Magan tried a prompt reply but groped for the right words, "Yes... but... not really, you know... here is this..."

Koli went inside taking the sacks from his hand and rested them on the floor in one corner, then gestured to Magan to seat himself.

Magan settled on a platform against the wall in the courtyard. Koli missed the last few words that Magan had uttered in confusion, "You were saying something..."

Magan hesitated a bit and then said after taking a deep breath, "I mean... There is something Girad wanted me to pass on to you. I came for that reason... nothing else."

Koli looked surprised and curious. "What? Girad wanted to pass on something to me! What is that?"

Magan pulled out a small pouch made of soft fabric and unfastened the knot at the opening of the pouch. Koli stared at the pouch with intense curiosity.

"This is it!" Magan was holding a necklace of bright red carnelian beads.

Koli was shocked at first and then her brows knotted in a frown of complete incredulity. She took the necklace from him and inspected the beads very closely for a long moment. After a thorough observation she mumbled, "It's very strange. I know this piece of ornament. This is an original piece and Girad used to keep this very carefully in a different packet. I heard him telling someone that he would manage a good price for this item. I can't imagine why he might send this to me!"

Magan regained his composure. "Oh! He said he wanted you to keep this as a memento."

Koli smiled sardonically, "Memento! Hmm... I don't buy that suggestion. Anyway, forget it. How is your life going on at the council?"

Magan relaxed a bit yet felt unhappy. His tongue had betrayed him.

"Going on well." Magan contemplated on how he could recover the lost opportunity.

Koli fiddled with the necklace with a puzzled expression, "Do you think there is a craze for such items in the nations beyond the ocean? Girad thought they would pay a fortune for jewellery like this. Here, though it's expensive, it is more or less within the reach of common people."

"Yes, Girad is right in my opinion. Unlike us, they have a clear distinction between classes. There exist a ruling class and the ruled. The ruling class enjoys most of the wealth and luxury. The remaining lot slogs and scrambles for the remnants. In addition, they are not very familiar with this technology. You see, many of our craftsmen are settled there. They manufacture this kind of bead according to the preferred design and shape. In fact, the trick of drilling the hole through the small bead is the catch. That's the secret. Since the market is restricted within the ruling class alone price realization is always good."

"Is there a lot of difference in the way the different classes live there?" Koli asked in curiosity.

Magan felt happy that he could elicit some interest; he went on, "Yes! That's not all. They don't limit the distinction within the realm of life alone."

"What do you mean?" asked Koli wide eyed.

"They distinguish the lives between classes even after death."

"And how is that?"

"The rich and powerful are buried with all sorts of mundane and luxury essentials in the grave! In fact, I heard they even bury the dead with arms, cooking pot and what not! Just imagine the dead body cooking its delicacies and fighting with other ghosts! I have heard that the royal tombs of the ruling class are truly spectacular. Can you imagine such a thing here? Hardly a few bangles, beads or a copper mirror might be buried with the dead. Otherwise, the fire takes it all. I feel that's much better. What do you think?"

"Of course, life is much more important than death," Koli observed.

"In the earlier days burial was even more ceremonious for the rich. Lately they are also starting to value the reality of life as we do."

Koli listened intently, but the expensive memento from Girad kept bothering her. She had felt that lately Girad almost hated her. This separation did not affect either of them beyond a sense bringing relief to both of them.

The council took care of the family's welfare during a merchant's sponsored ventures. Hence, she would have no problem surviving. Even in the absence of such assistance from the council, Koli could have survived with the resources left to her by her father.

Magan suddenly rose to his feet, "I shall take your leave."

Magan walked through the town in a trance repenting about his failure to achieve his goal. He never suspected that he would lose his nerve in front of the beautiful woman. Her disposition simply paralyzed his conscious designs.

He sat by the side of the road, ruminating. The bright noon mellowed into a pale afternoon and then a veil of dusk ran swiftly from one end of the horizon to the other. Magan remained lost in his aimless haze.

After a long time, he finally rose to his feet again and started walking in a hypnotic trance. His steps fell on the ground in a mechanical rhythm. Shortly, he found himself standing outside the gate of Koli's house. He knocked on the wooden door.

Koli came out with a candle at hand, "You!"

"Yes! I just wanted to confess that the necklace was not a memento from Girad. I bought it from him for you!"

Saying so, he turned on his heels and vanished into the darkness. Koli stood rooted at the door for a long moment, staring into the black void and then slowly went inside, closing the door.

24

The carpenter was looking for the right kind of wood for building the roof of a house. So long he had been making small value furniture or occasionally utensils. People preferred utensils made of burnt clay. For the first time, he got a contract for some construction work. But, to find such wood is not easy. It must be durable enough and able to withstand the vagaries of nature. He had started searching the suitable tree long back when it was noon. The sun was right above his head then. Now, it was almost evening. The sun had taken a dip beyond the horizon and a faint dying glow suffused the density of the forest. The increasing buzz of the exotic insects and variety of wild bushes made him conscious that he had come too far from civilized world. He decided to go back. He would scout again tomorrow for the desired wood. Only he must begin early.

On his way back, he planned to take a different and shorter route. He tried to walk hurriedly through the rapidly darkening forest. Suddenly a swarm of flies hummed around his head. He tried to swat them away but more flies appeared from nowhere. A sharp tingle at his neck made him shriek. He realized that it was not only a few harmless flies but a pack of wild insects flocked around him. In a panic he started to run. Abruptly, the dense foliage disappeared and he arrived in the middle of a little clearing among the trees. The sight in front of his eyes froze him in terror.

A goat was lying in a pool of some strange creamy liquid. Repulsive stench filled the air. He tiptoed near the motionless body of the goat tentatively. On a closer look, he realized that the goat's neck was pierced by some spear. Stream of blood oozed out through the cut. Apparently, the animal was then smeared with milk and honey to draw all sorts of wild insects around its decaying flesh.

The carpenter trembled in horror and revulsion. For a few moments he could not move. And then with a sudden start, he ran. His nauseated head drove his legs in frenzy. The entire forest seemed to gulp him into its grisly womb. Another gruesome sacrifice had been made! He must escape the gaming zone of some maniac.

25

"That's atrocious! Why did you do that?" Sindhu exclaimed in disbelief.

Magan sat with his head hung low. He had narrated the events of the previous day to Sindhu.

Sindhu was stunned at the mindless advance that Magan had made so abruptly. "It can evolve into a scandal, do you understand? She is fairly connected to the top echelons of the council. Moreover, at this point of time, she is always in discussion thanks to that thug's adventure. Could you not wait a few days and consult me before jumping around like a hero?"

Magan slowly lifted his eyes and mumbled, "I am in love with her."

Sindhu flung his hand in the air in frustration and mimicked bitterly, "I am in love! Anyone who comes across that woman falls in love with her. Even that thug did once upon a time. Your confession could have waited a bit and things might have been better. By the way, how did she react when you announced your real intention behind the gift?"

Magan remained mum for a long moment and then said, "I did not wait to check her reaction. I ran away from there as soon as I said it."

Sindhu thought for a while and spoke aloud contemplatively. "You know what? She is a very dignified woman, brought up by her father in a conservative manner. She may not respond to such advances. If she goes to the council and complains they would believe her and…"

"I don't care what the council does. If she rejects me I shall be broken forever."

"You are not in the right state of mind now. Relax and let me do something."

"What are you going to do?"

"I don't know. Maybe I shall meet her in the evening and try to find out her reaction. If she is upset and intends to involve the authorities, I shall convince her to ignore the whole episode. She may go to the council if she is frightened. She lives alone and it's a matter of her security. You better stay away from the upper town for a while. Don't complicate things."

"What security are you talking about? I am in love with her. I can't hurt her in any way."

"I know that, but what matters is what *she* thinks. I must find that out," said Sindhu.

"Okay then. I shall wait till you let me know your findings."

A messenger appeared and ordered both of them to see the council head right away. They hurriedly proceeded to meet him.

The council head was accompanied by a few other advisers.

"We have decided to start a new initiative." said the council head with an affable smile.

Sindhu waited expectantly.

The ruler said, "The divine secrets based on which the standards and customs of our land are built must be preserved. You already know a few of them; for instance, the significance of the number hundred and eight. If the secrets are lost for some reason, say an earthquake, or a military attack from beyond the ocean, or suppose the nomads from over the mountain slowly gather mass and enslave us, then what will happen? In fact our mighty rivers are also infamously unpredictable. We did build these towns over very high platforms. But another violent flood or a ruthless drought can destroy most of us. Then?"

Sindhu and Magan listened to the monologue in silence.

"Then all our legacy and traditions would be erased. If the secrets are not spread more widely among the masses, the risk of extinction remains very high. Hence, we must implement a certain strategy to educate our people about the reasons behind such practices."

An adviser added his comment, "I feel that we should be careful in this matter. I agree with you that we must create widespread awareness about these aspects, but there has to be a limit as to who can access this information. It should not be open for public consumption. A majority of the masses love magic."

Sindhu got the point of the argument and added, "Each of us loves to see supernatural effects. For example, our people worship womanhood because they find the emergence of life to be divine, well beyond human control. They find man to be a modifier or destroyer but it's only the female of all species that can create. For the masses it's an absolutely divine affair. Some of us do know the process and a bit of logic behind these things. If knowledge of this kind is made public, the divine status of womanhood will be impugned, and perhaps it will no longer be associated with Godhood. The respect for women in our society may dwindle.

"I state this as an example, to convey my concern that we should spread the secrets in a restrictive manner to restore the fabric of faith among people."

The ruler deliberated over the argument but held a different opinion, "I personally feel that blind faith and mindless rituals will not take us much ahead. The higher the level of intelligence and knowledge, the better would be the development of this civilization. However, if you people feel that we should keep the awareness limited at the moment, we shall do so. Now, let me tell you the initiative under consideration."

The ruler stopped for a while to consolidate the thoughts in his mind and narrated the list.

"We would like to create a secret community preferably consisting of a young lot for such awareness. We shall educate them in all our unique traits and legacies. We shall teach them the significance of the proportions and measurements employed all over this land."

One of the advisers suggested, "We must ensure that they learn the techniques of casting the alloy metal by heart. This must never be lost in the annals of history."

"Also the bead-making technology should be taught. It's true that the secrecy of the method has proved extremely profitable to us. Our people earn a hell of a lot of wealth by selling those ornaments, yet the small circle within which the knowledge is limited subjects it to the risk of extinction."

"What about the game of dice?"

"Well, it's unlikely to be lost because almost every household loves to play games and has a set of dice with them. We shall explain the symbolism of uncertainty in this nature that will keep reminding the human race about the lack of control over fate that man has. This will prevent them from assuming a sense of being almighty themselves."

"What about belief and faith?"

"Yes! We shall take care of that as well. For instance, we shall ingrain the significance of applying the holy red pigment on the narrow parting of the hair for women committed to specific men. Whatever is the religious reason behind the practice, it ensures a unique identity and sense of completeness in their appearance. Women from no other place pursue such a practice. This is kind of an identity card. I foresee that we shall not remain restricted within this geographical boundary forever. Some day our people will spread all over the earth and then I don't want them to lose their uniqueness and heritage."

"Some religious beliefs must continue. We worship fertility. Let's keep doing so. To keep the huge population united, at least one single God is indispensible."

"Hmm... one single God! That's a good idea, but then what happens to the rest of the gods and goddesses?"

"All will remain. We don't try to uproot faith, but the specially trained lot will be imparted with the intensive significance of the fertility God; the creator! The symbol of manhood and womanhood combined should continue to carry the legacy of our faith from generation to generation."

"I think we all agree with it. Over a period of time, we might end up with the memory of submission to this God and the others may fade away over time... Not a bad idea."

"Hence, it is final that we shall have a group of young learned people who will be trained in the legacies of our civilization. Now, don't we feel that we should issue a certification of accreditation to such people whom we train?"

"Of course, that's the other aspect. To do that, we require a very special symbol that can be etched on the seal of identity. So, gentlemen, what are the aspects you would like that symbol to convey?"

"Bonding."

"Secrecy."

"Enigma."

"Nested."

"Power."

"Mystery."

"Great! So, that's your job, Sindhu and Magan. Take your time and evolve a suitable symbol. Remember that the symbol must carry the said impressions. Shortly the religious festival season is going to start. We wish to start the implementation of the plan immediately after that; now focus on this mission. Think of the seal."

26

Koli generally collected her daily ration in bulk from the council at certain intervals. This helped her to avoid the hassle of visiting the council every day. She preferred to go in the morning and returned home before sunset. Today was an exception. She had been deeply engrossed in giving shape to a lump of clay the whole day, and she was imperceptive to the departure of morning and noon.

When she started out for the council, it was already late. By the time she made her way back home, dusk was falling rapidly over the dusty town. Shortly, the roads were dark and the flames of the torches flared up on the sides of the lanes. Though the council ensured that the torches were lit every evening, the life of such flames remained ephemeral on windy nights. They were snuffed out as soon as the wind struck its impish blow.

Koli sauntered through the lanes with two heavy sacks of groceries and other daily necessities in her over-strained arms. After making it halfway between her home and the council, she was struck be a sense of eeriness; as if footsteps softly fell on the ground in harmony with hers. The uncanny noiselessness of the footsteps distinguished themselves in the faint bustle of the road. The lane was not deserted, but was frequented by a thin crowd of passersby. Koli stopped immediately and turned to see the faces of the people walking behind her. Each face she scanned appeared perfectly innocent and oblivious to her existence on the road. She assured herself that it was nothing but an illusion. Stark loneliness made her slightly paranoid. The weird face at the window long ago had left an indelible impression on her memory. She tried to shrug the creepy feeling off and started to walk again.

A shadowy figure emerged out of a by lane and resumed stalking Koli. Over a period of time he had mastered the skill of treading like a cat. He could run soundlessly. Even the hiss of his flagging breath was imperceptible. He followed Koli from a modest distance. His eyes glued to the sinuous languidness of her gait. He admired everything about her. The suddenly alert suspecting eyes scouting for a predator stimulated his fascination. He drank the beauty of her flaring nostrils, her large black, watchful and slightly nervous eyes. Her diaphanous vulnerability veiled by a veneer of conscientious dignity appealed to his eyes drenched with obsessive longing. He felt like coming out in the open to envelop her existence with his loving embrace. But he could not afford to do so. The right moment was yet to come. He must wait. Yet, he never let his desirous gaze stray from Koli's body.

She walked briskly. Though she tried to discard the disturbing inkling of being followed by someone, yet the sensation remained at the back of her mind. Shortly, she again felt uneasy as if a pair of adamant eyes was glued to her existence. The footsteps were inaudible yet they never ceased to tap the ground. She again paused and whipped around to see the faces behind her. There was nothing unusual. Strangers walked by indifferently. But as soon as she resumed walking, the feeling returned. After every few steps, she turned her head to ensure that it was just an unfounded paranoia.

The shadowy figure wondered at his amazing intuition; he always seemed to know exactly when Koli would turn her head around. He could read her mind like an open book. He knew her so well, so intimately, like an undivided part of his own flesh and bones. He had never had the opportunity to be close to Koli. He had never witnessed the lithe bearing throbbing under the impassive layers of fabric. Yet, he felt as if he had spent a million nights with her. He had no doubt that she belonged to him and he belonged to her. Only, he could not afford to speak his mind. The time was not yet right. He did not feel as though he was invading her privacy. He knew that he was doing her a favour. It was late in the evening and the law and order situation in the town was not like it was a decade ago. It was not safe for her to travel alone. His watchful eyes kept her safe from any kind of danger that could be lurking on the way.

Koli rushed in a panic. Though she tried to believe that her sixth sense was unfounded, she was perpetually being flooded by uneasiness. Finally, she reached her home. Opening the door, she dropped the entire load on to the floor and sat on the dais to catch her breath. After her breathing returned to normal, she rose to her feet and picked up the groceries that she had collected from the council. At that moment it struck her that her identity seal was missing. She upturned all the sacks but could not find the clay tablet. She had been clutching it in her hand while walking from the council to her home. In her panic she had been oblivious of her surroundings and the seal might have slipped out of her hand. She was aghast! Without the seal, it was impossible to get the ration from the council. Getting a replacement involved a tedious bureaucratic process. She was in trouble.

Night had fallen and it was not possible for her to go back to look for the seal. She decided to go to bed, burying her worry for a while.

She rolled on her bed restlessly the whole night. The disturbance infiltrated every blink of sleep that she could attain. Finally, when the first rays of the morning sun trickled into her bedroom, she gave up the tortuous struggle to pretend to slumber.

She splashed her tired eyes with cold water. Koli always loved to watch the town when the sun emerged from the eastern horizon. She opened the main door to step outside.

Her feet brushed against something on the floor. She looked down and saw that it was the square clay seal! She was stunned. She had searched the entire porch the night before and had turned up nothing. But… but… the seal was now lying there on the floor, smiling a reassuring smile, illuminated by the morning rays.

27

Koli was delighted to see Sindhu standing at her doorstep. After Girad's departure, she was free and peaceful, but at times Koli felt the need for company. She realized that she needed people around her… even if they were enemies. Solitude came with too much silence. With a broad smile, she asked Sindhu to come inside.

"Who is bringing your ration from the council?" asked Sindhu with concern as he noticed Koli shaking her arm, apparently trying to shrug off some adamant pain. Neck pain was a chronic problem that haunted the population. Lifting and carrying heavy loads damaged the spinal cords of most of the populace.

"I bring it myself. Yes, my hand is paining. I brought two instalments of the supply last night. I don't like to go there frequently. On my way back, I could not find a cart. So, I had to walk all the way. It was indeed heavy. This hand has been hurting since noon. Anyway, it's unavoidable."

Sindhu listened with concern and said after contemplating briefly, "Don't bother. Give me the identity seal. I shall get it for you whenever your turn comes. You don't need to go there. You just let me know what you want."

Koli smiled in gratitude. "Are you sure? You are busy… will you be able to come here so often?"

Sindhu nodded. "I shall manage. Anyway, I go there every day. The distribution counter is just behind the room where we work."

"Do you work alone or are there others who work with you?" Koli asked casually.

"Yes I have a colleague. He helps me make the seals. He is very experienced and has been with the council for a longer period than me. His name is Magan."

"Magan!" Koli almost yelled in sudden excitement.

"Yes, is there anything special about him? You seem to be thrilled!" Sindhu said this provocatively.

Koli quickly checked her reactions, "Not at all!"

"I guess you had met him when the council was looking for the seal that was lost." added Sindhu.

Koli's face lit up as if she had located some forgotten image in her mind, "Correct. Someone came to ask about the seal. It was him… yes! He was a nice chap. He had just enquired about the seal and left. His face did not settle in my memory well. Now that you mention him, I can sort of recall him."

"Why? Did you not meet Magan when we went to see Girad off? He oversaw the entire execution along with me."

"Oh! Yes. He was there that day too… right."

Sindhu was a bit intrigued at this. Koli could not have forgotten the entire conversations with Magan. Magan had narrated the discussions, word by word, every time he had visited Koli.

Sindhu knew that Koli was not being transparent. Either she was inclined to respond to Magan's advances, or she simply wished to hide the scandalous development by waiving it off.

Suddenly Koli seemed to recall something. "Oh… I think he left something at my place when he had come to ask for the seal."

"What was it?"

"I can't remember now. I have to look for it. Why don't you request him to drop in at my place sometime? I shall locate the item and return it to him."

Sindhu nodded. He was at a loss. There was no doubt that Koli was suppressing something, but he could not guess the motive.

The subject of discussion changed.

"So, what are you working on nowadays?" asked Koli with a curious glint in her eyes.

Sindhu was delighted to talk on this subject. "It's an interesting thing. The council decided to form a special community. The members of that community will be educated about the secrets behind our rituals and traditions. They will be responsible to carry forward the traditions from one generation to the other."

"Can I be a part of such a community?" Koli asked eagerly.

"I guess so. That's the reason I came to see you. I can suggest your name as a prospective member."

Koli glowed with excitement, "That's great! How are you involved in it? You will be a member or a guide?"

"No, I remain the same — a seal maker. I am supposed to bring up the idea of a special emblem that will identify the members — a symbol that will invoke a sense of bonding, secrecy, mystery…"

Koli looked thoughtful, "Can I be of any help to you?"

"Sure you can, but this is supposed to be restricted to the select council members. If a good idea strikes you, let me know. It will be useful. Of course, I shall propose your name for membership in the prospective secret community."

"I shall tell you if I think of something. What about dinner? I have some good dry fish cooked for the night."

Sindhu smiled in gratitude, but refused to stay for dinner politely. He had already cooked his food before coming to Koli's place, and if left uneaten, the humidity and heat would decompose the food overnight.

Sindhu preferred to walk instead of being carried by a cart. It had been quite some time since he had been living in this town. He felt as if he had led two distinct lives: one discarded at the forgotten coastal town and the other in this thriving neighbourhood of Koli, her departed father, Girad and so many others.

The past life, though shed like an old tattered cloth, often came back, clouding his head. He had had parents, a life filled with the days of aimless fun of childhood. And, one day he had found himself to be completely alone, engaged in a struggle for survival. He had survived, but at a heavy cost. What bothered him even to this day was that he was still all alone.

As he meandered through the mud-brick lanes of the upper town, he made a bitter resolve that he would not give up, never! Nature had tried to kill him once, but had failed. He had survived and rose like a phoenix from the ashes - today he walked the earth like an unassailable ghost. Life tricked him into a riddle for the second time. He would surely outwit destiny. He would not remain alone forever. He would not live with only the memories of his loved ones for the rest of his life. His days of dry and sulking solitude would surely come to an end someday. He would emerge as the winner.

28

"Now this is getting on my nerves! How many samples did we make? Countless! Each one is rejected with a casual shake of the head by that bearded man!" Magan's flustered outburst startled Sindhu.

"Relax. This is a part of life. We can't afford a reaction like that. If you ask me, I am not sure that we could bring out our best yet. This seal is going to be a legendary mark in our history. It must be a special one. Don't lose patience," advised Sindhu, though he was himself tired of the number of attempts they had already made. The ruler always found something amiss with the symbol. If the sense of unity was evident, the impression of secrecy was missing. If it conveyed an aura of mystery, it lacked originality. It could never invoke the entire plethora of impressions that the council had demanded.

As they returned to their cell after meeting the ruler, Magan slouched on the platform, exhausted and morose.

"Come on, cheer up my friend." Sindhu tried to perk up his spirits.

Magan stared at the floor blankly for a long moment and then mumbled, "How can I cheer up? Life has come to a standstill for me. I cannot dare take a chance to meet her now."

Sindhu was alert at once, "You better not, I feel. When I met her, she never disclosed the fact that you had paid her a visit in the middle of that stormy night. In fact she feigned to be completely unfamiliar with you. But, she wanted you to visit her to hand the necklace back to you, most probably. But if you go there, you may be walking into a trap. One of the senior administrators of the council is her neighbour."

"It may be an invitation as well. Why do you think only negatively? She may be willing to take it forward."

"Maybe. I am not denying it. But I feel that you should wait for a few more days. I shall meet her shortly to deliver the requisite ration from the council. I will then tell her that you were too busy with work and could not make it. I want to watch her reaction. It will explain a lot. In addition, the religious festival will be starting in a few days. We shall get a grand opportunity to interact socially with everyone. At that time, you will anyway get a chance to meet her. It will be a public place and no trap can be laid there. I advise you to be patient. Everything will be okay"

Magan considered the advice. It sounded reasonable. Meeting Koli during a social gathering would be perfectly safe.

29

Koli headed to the market. The mysterious pouch held in her palm seemed to emit a disturbing pulse of eeriness. The strange feeling made her nauseous. The previous afternoon she had gone to the same market to look for some ornaments that she could wear during the upcoming festival. She had tried several shops, but none of the artefacts had captured her fancy. The designs were too flashy and loud, unlike the jewellery that was popular during her father's time. Married women donned all sorts of heavy stones all over their body. Koli felt that she would disappear from view if she enveloped herself with such elaborate embellishments. People would fail to notice her existence because the gold and carnelian beads would scream hoarse, stealing all the attention.

Finally, she had given up and to pacify her disappointment, she had randomly chosen a pair of simple golden bangles. She had suggested some modifications to be made on the existing design. The merchant promised to carry out the same and deliver it to her home the following day. She had made some advance payment and left.

Something peculiar had happened this morning. The merchant sent a boy to her home to deliver the bangles. She received the pouch and saw that the two bangles were modified as she wished. When Koli was about to make the payment, something drew her attention; in spite of taking the bangles out, the pouch did not seem empty. There was still something inside. She turned the pouch around and shook it. A necklace, a pair of earrings and another pair of bangles slipped out; they were exquisitely beautiful, the very embodiment of the designs she had always aspired for. They were not made of gold or some other expensive metal but were crafted from burnt brown clay. She could not take her captivated eyes off of them for a long moment; but soon her surprise turned into eeriness. She had never ordered the articles. In fact, it had never occurred to her that burnt clay articles were also to be had. How did they come into pouch?

"I think there is a mistake; I never ordered these items," She told the boy who had come to deliver the ornaments.

"I don't think so. I saw my master putting these clay items very consciously into that pouch. Also, he instructed me to collect the remaining payment for the gold bangles only."

"What do you mean? These clay items are free?"

"I don't know. But I am supposed to accept the payment only for the gold bangles."

"That's strange. Is he going to be there in the shop in the afternoon?"

"Yes. You can go and talk to him. I just follow orders."

So, Koli headed for the market. She needed an explanation. It was ridiculous that such uncommon pieces of ornaments had been sent to her for free. She arrived at the shop just before sunset.

"What is this? Why did you send these to me?" She demanded.

The merchant was busy with a few other clients, but excused himself for a little while to attend to Koli. "Oh! It must be a sweet surprise. You never asked for burnt clay jewellery. That's why I never showed them to you when you were here yesterday."

"Of course! Then why did you send these to me?"

The merchant looked slightly baffled, "Because they were paid in full and I was supposed to deliver them to you along with what you had ordered last evening."

"Come on, don't talk in riddles. When I never saw them yesterday, how could I have paid for them in full?" Koli was becoming impatient now.

"You did not pay but he paid. He also said that you were going to put on these clay ornaments during the festival."

Koli frowned in surprise, "Who is he?"

The merchant was now completely puzzled, "I don't know… I thought he was your husband!"

"My husband! What did he look like?"

The merchant was now in a fix. He met countless clients every day. Unless there was something typical about their disposition, he could not recollect them. "Look madam, I have a short memory. I can't recall exactly, but he was a middle-aged man with a dark complexion. He was slightly taller than you."

Koli was now flustered, "Almost every man in this town answers to that description!"

"Why can't he be your husband? I can recollect one thing. He was very sincere when he said that you would love those designs. He desperately wanted to please you. I guess you are upset with your husband for some reason, maybe thinking that he could not gift you such exquisite jewellery. You are wrong, he loves you a lot."

Koli ignored the merchant's babble and left the counter. Even though she wished for the pouch to be gone, she could not release it from her grasp. The question swirled inside her head like the deafening hum of bees: "Who was he?"

30

The morning rays rested idly on the floor. Koli sat on the floor, toying with the golden bangles and the complete set of burnt clay ornaments. The brown piece of art never stopped to fascinate her. The mystery shrouding the arrogantly simple set of necklace, earrings and bangles rendered them even more aristocratic. Though she felt the prickling eeriness of their inexplicable existence, somehow she fell in love with them.

She went into the bedroom and brought out the looking glass along with a little wooden box. She had never used the box in the past, although it was considered a sacrilege to stay away from it. It contained the blood red pigment that every married woman applied on the parting in her hair. Though she had received the box as a part of the marriage ritual from the priest, she had never used it.

This morning she toyed with the box for a long moment and then opened it tentatively. She combed her thick black hair and then parted it in the centre of her head.

Once she had had a vicious argument with Girad over this matter. Girad had demanded that she follow the custom adopted by every other married woman in the land. He also insisted that Koli carry out the elaborate ritual of worshiping the animal god. She had shrugged off the suggestions sneeringly.

Koli adamantly stayed away from all kinds of rituals and

traditions. When provoked enough, she declared that it was stupid to segment nature under a complete hierarchy of deities. She argued that each god being omnipotent, could not be defeated by the other and hence devoting oneself to a particular god conveniently resulted in segregating the social fabric into bits and pieces. In her view, one could not fight nature, or protect oneself from nature, because mankind was a part of nature itself. Worshipping the fire god or the rain god meant taking sides of one over the other. Nature did not fight with itself. Then why must she worship any of the gods? She was herself an embodiment of nature. She did not see reason in prayer.

Similarly, she did not feel the need to flaunt her marital status. A thin trace of red pigment on her hair-parting did not help her realize the commitment to her marriage; neither did its absence alienate her from her family. She adamantly refused to follow the custom. Girad was appalled at her unconventional behaviour, but could do nothing about it. All he could do was hate her for it.

This morning, out of mere fancy, she poured that fine dust of the red pigment onto her hair-parting. Due to her lack of experience, she ended up smearing the powder over a large area on her head. Yet, in the mirror she found herself looking strikingly different from her usual appearance. Inside the room, it was relatively dark, though a slice of sunlight illuminated a part of the floor. She collected the clay ornaments and went out to the veranda to check herself in the mirror under bright rays of the sun.

Koli stood under the clear, open sky and looked at the mirror with the sun facing her. The bright red patch on her countenance seemed to have given her a complete makeover. She seemed more attractive than ever. Some of the red pigment had smeared over her forehead. Koli looked ravishing. Mesmerized, Koli stared at her reflection for an eternity, until she heard a thud coming from the back of her house. She was jolted back to consciousness. She put aside the clay ornaments on the ground and went to check the source of the strange noise.

The backyard was empty. There was no trace of any fallen object. She came back to the veranda in a confused state. She shook her head and decided to wear the clay necklace and earrings. As soon as she glanced at the clay articles, her blood froze. They were lying on the veranda, scattered and smashed into bits and pieces. Someone had just destroyed them with a heavy object!

The shadowy figure rushed through the lanes in a rage. He was breathing heavily, more from agony than from exhaustion. Koli's appearance, ornate with the glaring redness of the holy pigment had struck his eyes, mocking him. He desperately wanted to tear the vision away from his view but could not. As he tried to chase it away, it laughed at him derisively from a distance. He could only smash the clay ornaments he had sent the previous evening. Koli could not belong to someone else… she could not put on that bloody pigment! She had never done so before. He felt as though he were burning in hell fire as he stomped over the baked brick lanes.

31

"The head-priest has sent his blessings for you three brave hearts," announced the old man in white beard.

"We follow his dictate blindly…that's it."

"Of course, that's what I am supposed to ensure. You see, our sacrifices have paid off. We have been able to fend off the disaster until now. We never know what is in store for tomorrow. We must listen to him." The old man sounded enigmatic.

"Why do you say that? We have always been following him without question. In fact, the rituals, though horrid, were performed unswervingly."

"True. You did all that. And almost every soul in the town is aware of this. Only they don't know who is carrying out those holy sacrifices. Our job becomes a bit challenging now."

"You are talking about the alert citizens we guess…right?"

The old man let out a brief laughter, "Partially right. Everyone is careful about his cattle. It is going to be increasingly difficult to whisk away some cow or goat from the herd. But the challenge is somewhere else…you see."

The three young men stared at him quizzically.

"Everyone in this town, including the ruler is suspecting the obvious."

"Yes…everyone is talking about the head priest's involvement in this. I hope, he understands that we have no role to play in spreading this rumour…correct?"

"He is a very understanding man. Don't worry about that. He wants us to carry out something more to seal the ill fate of our settlement. I think, the town is ready for it. Everyone is expecting it to happen any time now."

The three men exchanged nervous glances with each other and one of them uttered in a whisper, "Do you mean a human sacrifice?"

The old man nodded. "Yes! Now, the town will not be shocked if they discover a few sacrificed bodies of healthy men in their early youth. All over the town, every other person is talking about it. Though they sound nervous about it, I know they want it done. And you are the men with guts."

The three men fell silent. After a long moment, they said, "We shall do it. But when and how?"

The old man instantly raised his hand imperatively, "I shall tell you. Only, this time, I advise you to prepare the folks for this."

"How do we do that?"

"Go and casually spread the rumour that a couple of men are going to be sacrificed. Also, convey that the ancient tradition of ritual would be followed."

"Do you mean...we shall execute our subjects with similar cruelty?"

"Come on! It is not cruelty but mercy. Those fortunate animals and men are destined to be dedicated to the lord!"

"Okay. We shall spread the words, and you will guide us about our next step."

32

"Would you mind watching this show on your own for a while? I shall go and look for Magan. He will be around here somewhere," Sindhu told Koli. They had come to the annual festival.

Koli agreed. "That's fine, I shall watch this. This is my favourite show. Don't forget to tell Magan that I want to see him."

"Sure. That's the main reason I am going to try and fish him out of this crowd," Sindhu said smiling. He was about to leave, but stopped. He stepped close to Koli and stared into her eyes with an impish grin. Koli looked baffled and gazed at him quizzically.

"Magan is a nice man, you know." Sindhu said teasingly.

Koli quipped, "I guess so," keeping up the mischievous tempo.

"You are a nice woman." Sindhu was smiling broadly now.

"Umm… that's also true." Koli played along.

"Girad is a bit crazy."

Koli pretended to ponder and nodded thoughtfully, "I am afraid so… Yes."

Sindhu chuckled, "Hmm… I shall go and get Magan for you now …. By the way, we must ensure that we remain in a group. People are talking about human sacrifice. You never know who becomes the victim. I shall get back soon. Wait here."

Koli leaned against a wooden pillar supporting the big structure of the stage and watched the show. A young girl danced to the tune of a folk song. Koli enjoyed this tradition. It was the typical art form of a particular tribal community. The young dancer generally performed the dance with very little clothing, though the arms were usually covered with numerous bangles. The bangles seemed like they would jam the movement of the arms, yet the swift and rhythmic swinging of the arms always amazed Koli. She liked the catchy tunes as well.

Sindhu lightly tapped Magan on his shoulder. A magician was performing a trick. There was a die on the ground. The magician drew the crowd's attention by pointing at the lone die sitting on the ground. The crowd gave its affirmation in a chorus; there was no dispute over the magician's claim. He slowly covered the die with a clay pot and chanted a few magic words with his eyes closed. The crowd waited in suspense. After a few moments of pin drop silence, the magician lifted the pot slowly. There were three dice sitting on the ground now. Excited cheers and hoots burst like thunder from the crowd. Then the magician offered a mischievous smile in the general direction of the crowd and moved ahead with his next performance.

Magan was deeply involved in the show. He did not pay attention to the first round of taps on his shoulder. Sindhu whispered his name into his ear and Magan turned around startled.

"Yes? Oh you are already here!" Magan exclaimed.

"Yes I am. Did you like the magic?"

"Yes. I liked it."

"I think there is more magic in store for you today… better than this!" Sindhu said enigmatically.

"What do you mean?"

"Someone is dying to meet you!"

"Meet me!" Magan looked expectant.

Sindhu paused briefly to enjoy Magan's nervous anticipation. He said cryptically, "You know, there is a lady named Koli! Right now she is desperate to see you. I guess she does not intend to hand you over to the authorities because of your adventure in the middle of the night. She is in good humour... perhaps in a romantic mood! Come on, follow me!"

Magan jumped in excitement and started running.

"Hey! Don't run because I am not running. Where are you heading to? You have to follow me; I shall not follow you. Hold your excitement till you meet her. I might be wrong, as I told you only what I had guessed."

They arrived at the place where the dance was going on.

"Koli, here he is," Sindhu said with a mischievous grin.

Koli swung around, "Hey! How busy *are* you? I had requested so earnestly that I wanted to meet you, but you never turned up."

Magan absorbed every word with a broad smile, but could not find a suitable excuse or reply. He remained silent.

Sindhu came to his rescue, "We are busy working on a very special assignment ordered by the council. I told you about that. Magan is the main man behind the ideation process, you know."

Koli smiled in admiration.

Magan asked, "Did you like the dance show?"

"Yes, I did," Koli replied.

"A lot of different sorts of entertainment is available. Don't miss anything. I just saw some great magic!"

Sindhu craned his head and looked over the heads in the crowd. "I think there is an exhibition of exotic pottery over there. Many of them are imported by the merchants from beyond the ocean and over the mountains. You don't always see them in the market. Let's go and take a good look. What do you think Koli? You were once fascinated with such pottery, if I remember correctly."

Koli thought for a while and shook her head diffidently. "No. I want to watch the entire dance show. I have liked it since I was a child; I can't miss it. I shall not go anywhere. By the way, Magan I have something to talk to you about. When you are free, just let me know. Don't run away."

Magan said, "I never run away."

Koli held his eyes in an icy stare, "But, you did once and left something behind."

Sindhu pulled at Magan's hand and they left for the pottery exhibition.

It was a rich collection. Next to it, Ridham had his own stall of exotic jewellery from various parts of the world. Large crowds of women were gathered around his stall. He made good business capitalizing on the fascination in their eyes.

Ridham asked another man to take care of the stall and decided to join Sindhu and Magan.

"How is business?" asked Sindhu.

"Very good! I earned enough for the entire duration of the festival. The fee of participation has been recovered. I want to have some fun now."

"Then come with us." Sindhu replied.

As they approached the spot where the dance show was going on, Koli's voice interrupted them. Magan and Sindhu turned around and saw that Koli was animatedly calling them to draw their attention to something. They proceeded in that direction.

"Look at that." Koli said excitedly, pointing at a little gathering.

Sindhu and Magan approached to look at what had caught Koli's interest. A snake charmer was perilously playing with a lethally venomous snake. Each time the snake tried to hit the target in ferocious vengeance, the man sprang back swiftly to stay out of its reach.

"That's not great! There is no venom left in the snake – the poisonous fang has been plucked out. Come on, let's go." Ridham commented sneeringly. His voice was loud enough for the crowd to hear. The man playing with the snake heard it as well. In a sudden reflexive move, he grabbed the snake by its neck and turned around to see who had made the comment.

Ridham fell silent but watched with a challenging look in his eye. After a prolonged silence, the snake charmer said in a fit of resentment, "If you are so confident, will you dare to take a little bite of this cute reptile? Come on…"

No one volunteered.

After a brief moment, the snake charmer suddenly caught sight of a mouse scurrying along. As soon as it reached within his arm's length, he caught the mouse with his free hand. Looking at the crowd, he said with a cynical glimmer in his eyes, "See what happens when this mouse is bitten by the snake here."

The snake was released and so was the terrified mouse. At a slight cue from the snake charmer, the snake snapped at the mouse in the blink of an eye. It took only a few seconds for the mouse to plunge into the silence of death.

The snake charmer removed the lid of the basket. The crowd took a quick peek into the contents and a shiver ran through the entire gathering around him. The basket was full of the slithering bodies of reptiles coiled around each other. A few sleek snakes tried to slip out through the slight opening, but the snake charmer quickly pushed them down and closed the lid. "Each of them is powered with venom lethal enough to kill an elephant in a few seconds. If any of you still have a trace of doubt, you are welcome to verify for yourself. They are eager to demonstrate their evil prowess."

The crowd watched frozen in terror and sadistic pleasure. No one moved. Only Koli whispered to Sindhu.

Sindhu turned his eyes slowly in her direction and thoughtfully gazed into her eyes for a long moment. Then a faint smile crossed his lips, "You are a genius!"

Koli said abstractedly, "There cannot be a more apt symbol for what you are trying to represent."

Magan stood behind them and hesitantly asked, "What are you talking about?"

They slipped away from the crowd and found a relatively private corner to talk among themselves.

Sindhu spoke, "I had shared the motive of our assignment with Koli sometime back, and she has come up with a grand idea."

Magan looked at him quizzically.

"I sneaked a peek into that container and saw the jumbled mass of coiled snakes. It was a feeling of awe and terror; a strange sense of enigma... I don't know how to express it..." Koli stopped halfway unable to convey the overwhelming feeling sweeping through her mind.

Magan listened meditatively and after a long moment slowly nodded his head. He spoke in a low voice, "You are right... this will lead us to the right impression for the seal that we are working on."

Sindhu added as an afterthought, "But we need to take a closer look at the snakes for a longer period of time. Only then we can conceive of an idea..."

"How can we do that?" questioned Magan.

"We have to somehow get that basket from the snake charmer for some time so that we can have a long look at it." Sindhu suggested.

Magan trembled at the idea, "Come on! That's madness! I am not going anywhere near the snakes. It's an appalling idea!"

"That fleeting glance will not do, Magan. We must find a way," Sindhu had made up his mind.

The crowd had now dispersed and the snake charmer was gathering up his things. He had been performing the show for a long time, since the morning. As it was performed out in the open, without any arena, ungrateful spectators could easily get away by watching it for free. A few conscientious viewers paid whatever they wished. That comprised the snake charmer's earnings. Ridham went close to him and tentatively tapped him on his shoulder. The man turned around. Ridham's broad and deliberate smile welcomed him.

"Yes? I guess you are the one who had made that careless comment," the snake charmer said tersely.

Ridham was slightly deterred, but managed to regain his composure quickly "Ah… Yes. It was me, but I am now convinced and highly impressed with your skills."

"What do you want now other than a live test of the venom?"

"Nothing of the sort. I want to offer you something."

"Offer me? What? People only cheat me by not paying me their dues, but taking pleasure in my shows."

"I have an idea. Listen, I am a merchant myself. I am here in this land for a while. Shortly I shall venture out for the world beyond the ocean. Why don't you join me?"

"Join you?" The snake charmer was now apprehensive, but tempted.

"Yes, join me. I am a rich merchant dealing in various articles like gems and jewels, cotton, clothes, dry fruits etc. I have a stall here as well. When I go, I shall take you and your precious reptiles along. When you hold your show, you generally have no control over the visitors; they generally comprise of a floating crowd. But if you are attached to me, I can demand an extra price to those customers that would be interested in some entertainment after shopping. This will serve as an added attraction for my stall and result in a fixed income for you. Both of us together will be able to pull in a much bigger crowd than if we work separately. In fact, for you it will be a great advantage, as you can ensure that you will get paid for your shows. The only thing is that you will have to share a part of your earning with me. I shall also organize an enclosed space for you to conduct your show in."

The snake charmer listened attentively and finally seemed to appreciate the idea. He agreed.

As they concluded the deal, Ridham happened to catch sight of Magan, Sindhu and Koli. Earlier he had not noticed Koli properly. After quickly appraising her, Ridham called out, "Sindhu, come here! I have made a grand deal with my new friend."

All three had noticed the animated conversation between Ridham and the snake charmer, and were afraid that another loose comment would ensure that Ridham would be bitten!

Sindhu came running at his invitation.

"We have a deal..." Started Ridham at a loud voice so that everyone could hear, but quickly lowered his voice, "Who is that beauty? You never mentioned you knew such a woman! You know I love full buxom figures."

Sindhu asked, "Do you like her?"

"Of course! She has a lovely body; a goldmine of lust; and you know I am insatiable! We can compensate each other," remarked Ridham lecherously.

"Right! You can, but she happens to be a very respectable woman with connections in the council. Her father was a veteran seal-maker."

"Whom does she live with? Hope not the old god-dammed father."

"No…"

"Then? Who is the lucky man?"

"Well… it is difficult to ascertain if the man was lucky or not."

"What do you mean? Is he dead?" asked Ridham with a twinkle in his eyes.

"The man has gone beyond the ocean in search of fortune. He is a merchant."

"I see. How long has it been?"

"Not long."

"May I know the name of that person?"

Sindhu paused and considered sharing the fact, "You know him. His name is Girad!"

"Don't tell me that Girad had the option to sleep with this woman, but he quenched his fire with those sluts most nights!"

"Yes, exactly so."

"Then it is good news that he has left on a voyage. It takes almost a lifetime to return. Nobody knows better than I do. So, what's her name?"

"Koli."

"Hey, you simply introduce her to me; I shall manage the rest."

"I told you about her high station in the town. It's your choice if you want to risk your prospects."

Ridham burst into boisterous laughter, "You worry too much about others, my friend. Conscience and honesty will not take you very far."

"Well, I would like to inform you that you have a rival."

"Rival! Who the hell is that?"

Sindhu said, "Look there. Come, let me introduce you to him."

Magan and Koli were talking to each other in a muffled voice. Magan was eager to please her. Koli was smiling and appeared to insist on something. Magan nodded his head in abject obedience.

As they noticed Sindhu and Ridham approaching, they stopped their conversation. Sindhu introduced Ridham to the others and said, "I think we have gotten an easy solution to our problem."

Each of them stared at his face questioningly.

Sindhu said cryptically, "The snakes now belong to my friend here."

Ridham protested, "Ahh... What do you want from the snakes? Moreover, the snakes are not mine; it's just a deal with that man, a business contract."

"I understood, but you can always favour us by sharing that basket for a short while. Can't you convince your partner?"

Ridham pondered and asked suspiciously, "But why?"

"Because we want to take a long look at the jumble of slithering snakes in the confined space. We are working on an assignment given to us by the council. The details cannot be shared at the moment."

Magan was excited, "We don't want to keep the basket for a long time. Just a day will be good enough. Anyway, I am very scared of snakes. They are repulsive, yet the basket holds the clue to our riddle."

"Okay, not a big issue. I shall have to bargain with this snake charmer," Ridham said. After some consideration, Ridham went back to the man and suggested that he would let him keep all of his earnings on the next day of the fair, if he allowed Ridham to keep the basket of snakes for one day. The snake charmer agreed hesitantly. The basket was brought to them.

The afternoon was fading fast and evening setting in. A thin veil of dusk fell over the busy bustle of buyers and sellers. The crowd started to amble away.

Koli said, "I must go home now. It's late."

"Do you think you can go alone?" Magan asked with concern.

"Yes I can." Assured Koli with conviction, discarding any further deliberation on that subject and left.

Ridham proposed, "Why don't we celebrate this evening with some psychedelic drink?"

Sindhu considered the idea and nodded, "I don't mind though I am not much of a drinker, and Magan has never drunk anything beyond water before!"

Magan looked away shyly. He had indeed never had a psychedelic drink in the past and hence was uncertain.

Ridham watched him with a glint of mischief in his eyes, "Why don't you start tonight? I guess you had a nice afternoon with that buxom beauty, while we broke our heads over the bunch of repulsive snakes."

"Ahh… Magan, come on! He is a friend." Sindhu teased with an impish grin.

"I am afraid you people are referring to my brief talk with Koli, right?" Magan asked blushing.

"Of course, young man. What else? You are the lucky one!" Ridham said, smiling broadly.

"Can we start the drinking session? I shall drink tonight." Magan did not mind the veiled reference to his conversation with Koli.

"Yes!" both Ridham and Sindhu yelled in unison.

"What happens to the basket of snakes?" asked Sindhu nodding in its general direction.

"I shall carry that. Do you want it tonight?" Ridham asked.

Magan replied, "Not tonight. But who will take it home?"

Ridham replied, "Neither of us will do so I guess. This horrid basket will not make a good bed companion, I guess. I shall hide this somewhere around the inn where we shall drink. I know some locations behind that shop where we can hide it. They dump all the garbage there; it will not be noticed by anyone until tomorrow afternoon. We can collect it tomorrow morning.

They left for the inn where the psychedelic drink made from barley was served along with roasted dry fish. Ridham hid the basket in one corner of the dump yard and ensured that the lid was tightly closed.

Once settled with their goblets of drink, Magan said, "I hate snakes! I don't know how I shall manage to watch the reptiles. I can't imagine one of them slithering out and…"

Ridham promptly replied, "I shall help you. I know how to handle snakes. Indeed, they are poisonous. Hence the job is tricky, yet I think, I can manage. By the way, nothing comes for free in this world; everything has a price, my dear."

Magan looked at him questioningly.

"Hmm… You must introduce me to that woman," Ridham said.

Magan did not reply and stared at Ridham warily.

Ridham understood that the proposed deal did not sit well on Magan. He quickly changed the connotation, "Huh! Don't mistake me. I understand she is connected to the council in some way. I want some help from the council, that's all."

Magan dismissed the possibility. "If you need something from the council, ask Sindhu. Even I may be of direct help rather than Koli."

Sindhu was afraid that the exchange was heading towards a bitter conflict. He never trusted the drink. Moreover, Magan, especially, had no prior experience of gulping the somnolent spirit. He changed the subject abruptly. "Don't you think we are losing stability over the years? The river has been so very unpredictable lately."

The drink started to work and the discussion changed course at Sindhu's slight fiddling.

"I think so. Look at this platform; when it was constructed, people found it crazy that the town was going to be built at such a height; but you see, today it seems to be inadequate. We shall be buried under the pile of silt if there are a few more floods. What do you think Magan? Or you think only about those heaving breasts?" Ridham teased again.

Magan said, "I think about both. Anyway, we have survived with the danger for such a long time. We shall keep on doing so."

The conversation went on and picked up momentum as the drink flowed through their veins.

"Another round!" shouted Ridham majestically. He was already high. To Sindhu's surprise, Magan kept pace as well, though he was getting more drunk with every swig. He seemed to enjoy the high. The terseness between him and Ridham was diluting.

Suddenly Magan started to smile. His smile grew broader quickly.

Sindhu was sober because he had not drunk as much as the other two. He poked Magan with his elbow. But Magan ignored him. The smile was frozen on his face.

"Hey, what is making you smile like that?" asked Ridham.

Magan did not reply, but kept smiling.

Sindhu took a close look at his face and said, "Are you okay? Listen, I shall leave now. I am through for the night."

Magan now looked at Sindhu squarely, his eyes twinkling, "You did not ask what she said to me..." Magan said, holding up the suspense.

Sindhu stared at him curiously, but silently forbade him to speak any more in front of Ridham.

Magan ignored his warning and said, "She invited me to her home...!"

"Really!" exclaimed Sindhu.

"Yes! I am going to meet her tomorrow evening," announced Magan proudly.

Sindhu smiled indulgingly and suggested that they have one more round of drinks.

The drinks arrived and they finished the content in a single long gulp.

Putting down the burnt clay goblet, Sindhu rose to his feet, "I shall leave now. One more drop of drink and I shall collapse right here. Magan, I guess you should follow me. You have drunk enough."

Magan shook his head vehemently, "I am not leaving. I shall drink many more rounds. I am not drunk now. If at all, I was drunk in the afternoon when Koli smiled at me. This liquid is nothing... Aah... Let me sink into tomorrow's dream. Listen everyone, I am in love! And, she does not mind!"

"You can sink in to your stupid dream once you are home. You have no experience with this drink. This can completely paralyze your rationality. You are already talking nonsense. Come, I shall take you home." Sindhu stretched his arm inviting him to take it and follow.

Ridham intercepted, "Why are you so nervous? I am there. I shall take care of him. And I can tell you that Magan is perfectly steady. He can have a few more drinks and then I shall ensure that he reaches home safely. I am not as bad as one would think looking at my face!"

Sindhu laughed and gave up, "Okay then! But for me this is enough. I wish both of you a very good evening. I must leave now. Bye!"

Sindhu staggered out of the place and headed for the lower town. He was feeling sleepy. He knew that his capacity to hold his drink was limited and did not allow himself to cross the limit. He was satisfied. Finally, the day had been fruitful. Koli's idea was really dramatic. That would surely serve the purpose of the council. He had already planned a logo in his mind resembling the coiled snakes.

33

A tall burly shadowy figure dragged Magan's half conscious body over the gritty path leading to the quarters of the lower town allocated to the workers of the council.

The midnight silence was ruptured by the gravels grinding over the mud brick surface. Magan tried to clutch at his benefactor, but immediately fell into another spell of drunken stupor.

The burly figure breathed hard in exhaustion while supporting Magan's weight. Though the man knew the address tentatively, yet the route was not very clear, and the torches by the side of the road had ceased burning long ago. The entire stretch was washed in darkness.

As they finally stood in front of the door, the man laid Magan on the ground and shook his shoulder. Magan opened his bleary eyes.

"Open the door," the man said in a huff.

Magan stared blankly for a long moment and then raised his hands. Fumbling blindly about the latch, he could finally open the wooden plank that served as a door for the room.

The burly man grabbed him again and pulled the slumped body inside the room. He left Magan near the door and opened the only window in the room to provide some ventilation. Standing over his comatose body, the man stared at him for a few moments and then left quickly.

The door was ajar and the window open. It was a windy night, with a full moon dazzling in the sky. White light fell on the ground slicing through the darkness.

A rustling sound somewhere in the room tried to penetrate through Magan's slumber. He stirred feebly. Somewhere in the dark corner of the room, two fingers were dexterously at work. A basket's lid was lifted slightly and a stick fiddled around within. A bunch of slithering bodies came to life. The expert hand indicated and allowed one of them to escape the confines of the basket. The stick guided its movement skilfully. Its scaly texture glistened as it wriggled over the area on the floor lit by the shining moon.

Magan felt thirsty and some unusual noise, though feeble, interrupted his stupor. He turned to one side and tried to reach for the jug of water unconsciously. As he moved his hand, it fell on a moving object that suddenly jerked him half awake. He opened his eyes, still sunk in a haze of blankness.

The vision that flashed in the shining moonlight startled him out of his haze, but the erstwhile drunken stupor did not allow him agility. Magan stared at the flaring hood of the snake in front of him. First he thought it was a terrible nightmare, and tried to blink away the haze. But the snake did not offer him a breather to deliberate. Soon he was almost convinced about the reality of the flaring snake with its slightly swaying hood. He tried to move, but a lethal strike hit him on the face with desperate ferocity. Magan shrieked in pain and clasped his face in terror. As he tried to spring back, the snake raised its head once again and struck Magan on that hand that covered his face. Terror and excruciating pain paralyzed Magan and he passed out.

A pair of glaring eyes watched as the venomous snake bit Magan a few more times, digging its fangs all over his face and hand. Blood trickled out and formed a dark glistening blob on the floor.

Once the snake was sure to have slain its prey, it tried to slither away but a stick came to life once more. The snake was again guided by the stick to get back to its original abode, the basket. The lid of the basket was closed. After a few moments, the basket was on its way out of Magan's room.

34

It is very unfortunate and sad that we have lost one of our youngest and most talented artists." observed the ruler solemnly.

The assembly remained silent.

The ruler spoke again, "We believe he died of snake bite in his own quarter. It looks like an accident, but we cannot rule out the possibility of murder...or…" The ruler fell silent midway. He decided to avoid talking about what he actually believed. It must have been the first human sacrifice almost in the same manner as that goat in the forest…the terrible ancient way.

There was a feeble murmur among the assembled members. No one spoke aloud but waited in suspense.

"Yes. We do suspect that there are anti-social elements looking for the secret design of the seal. They want to have their counterfeit copy. Magan and Sindhu had been working on this mission as you all are aware."

Everyone listened in rapt attention.

The ruler continued, "We have reasons to believe that Magan was in touch with a merchant who harboured malicious intentions of sneaking the motif away from him. The alleged merchant might have threatened Magan, but ironically, Magan was not privy to the final theme. It was conceived by his co-artist who was yet to share the concept with him. When the thug realized that his identity was exposed to the wrong person, he killed Magan so that a fresh hunt could be carried out."

"Do we have any suspects? Who could the assailant be?" Someone asked.

"Yes. We have a hint. There is no proof, but we shall closely observe the movements of the alleged merchant for a while until we are sure of his guilt or innocence."

"What about the co-artist? His life is in danger as well."

"We shall send a group of sentries to guard him at all times, but covertly. This merchant will definitely choose him as his next target. The killer should not get an inkling that he is under surveillance. Don't worry; we shall close the snare very soon."

"What about the vacant position? Should we not appoint a new artist in Magan's place?"

"We shall do so over a period of time. The new man will not be necessarily involved in the secret mission. Only time can show the loyalty of a man. In addition, I feel, we can finalize this motif. This is the latest version that was proposed to me last evening. I feel this fits our purpose perfectly in all respects. Please take a closer look."

Everyone poured over the large clay tablet placed on the ground.

The engraving showed several snakes entwined with one another. The closely coiled snakes oozed an aura of mystery mixed with a sense of inhibition. It seemed to represent the symbol of a closely guarded clandestine society.

After a moment of awed silence, a consensus was asked about the appropriateness of the symbol. After a brief discussion the symbol was approved.

"We must reward the artist whose genius mind has conceived this unique idea." announced the ruler.

The council agreed unanimously.

35

With an elated spirit, Sindhu left his place of work, but he could not savour the pleasure of success to its fullest. Magan's death had cast a dark shadow on his mind.

He still wanted to share his excitement with someone and in Magan's absence, he could think of only one person – Koli. He also felt indebted to her for coming up with the idea of depicting the snakes in the seal. However, he could not risk disclosing this fact to the council. They had been sworn to secrecy. The council would not excuse him for this violation. It would also complicate Koli's life unnecessarily.

Sindhu could only convey his gratitude to her and nothing more.

"The council appoints you as the private adviser to the ruler from this day. This is a reward for designing the unique seal to validate the identity of the members of the privileged secret society." The announcement resounded in Sindhu's mind. He felt honoured and happy.

The council was closed the next day, as everyone wanted to relax. Three guards were assigned the duty to guard Sindhu. The council feared for his safety. These guards stayed with him always, breathing down his shoulder. He hated this interference but could not protest. Privacy was of vital importance to him. He felt that it prevailed over his own safety. In addition, he did not want the council to know that he had visited Koli, as it might drag Koli under suspicion. So he talked the guards into leaving him alone for the evening.

He suggested that they spend the evening with their families and assured them that this slight lapse would not be reported to the council. The guards left feeling obliged.

Sindhu threw a furtive glance around him to be sure that nobody was watching him as he neared Koli's house. Turning the bend in the alley, he froze! Koli's door was visible from the end of this alley.

Koli was standing at the open door seemingly seeing off someone. Sindhu saw the man from behind and instantly recognized him. It was Ridham. He could not think of any reason why Ridham would pay Koli a visit! Sindhu was alert at once as the council had appointed guards to watch Ridham's movements. He was a suspect in connection with Magan's death.

Sindhu quickly hid behind the wall of a house and waited for Ridham to leave. Ridham left shortly. After he disappeared around the corner of the alley, Sindhu emerged.

Running a nervous eye around him, Sindhu approached Koli's door.

"Why did Ridham come to meet you?" demanded Sindhu nervously as soon as Koli opened the door and let him in.

Koli's face glowed in delight, "See what I bought from him! Somebody told him that I am the daughter of a rich father who had left me a fortune! So he came to show his stock of goodies to me. I tell you, he is going to run out of business very quickly. Look at this!"

Sindhu looked at the bangle that Ridham had just sold. The bright red faience bangle had various kinds of jewels embedded all over its red surface. It looked very exotic. After inspecting it, Sindhu asked how much Koli had paid for the bangle.

Koli was thrilled because Ridham had sold it for a pittance.

Sindhu listened and sat there wondering about Ridham's motive. Ridham was not a fool. He would not spare a single item without earning a decent profit. Sindhu feared the worst. Ridham had made lewd remarks about Koli, the afternoon before Magan's death. Recalling that day, Sindhu remembered the lecherous gleam in Ridham's eyes when he had been eyeing Koli. The purpose of his visit instantly flashed in Sindhu's mind. Without any comment, he put the bangle aside.

Koli was effervescent, "He is a strange man. He saw me only once but spoke as if he has known me for ages. You know, he is widely travelled! He has seen the world beyond the mountain and sailed across the ocean for an uncountable number of days. Now he is back only for a short while before he embarks on to his next voyage. What an adventurous life he leads!"

Sindhu listened and commented, "So, it looks like you are highly impressed with him!"

In a fit of excitement, Koli replied, "Yes I am. Only one thing about him made me a little uncomfortable. But that is perhaps my habitual misgiving about every man lately."

"What is that?" Sindhu anticipated the inevitable.

"He admired me time and again within this short spell of time! He was not familiar with me till now and I found it bit disquieting."

"So, he found you stunning, I guess." said Sindhu tersely.

Koli laughed, "Yes he did. In fact, he declared that he had never come across such an appealing beauty in his lifetime even in the faraway lands!"

"And you fell for his phony words!" Sindhu was irritated.

Koli giggled, "Who does not like being flattered? I am a human being after all. Why should I not cherish such rhapsody? Only I could feel his hovering eyes over me at times, but he sold me the bangle at such a throwaway price!"

Sindhu was not amused. It worried him. He did not partake in Koli's exuberance about Ridham.

The rest of the evening was spent in discussing Sindhu's new role in the council and Magan's mysterious death. Both of them contemplated the obvious possibility of a human sacrifice. Sindhu did not subscribe the ruler's view that Magan had been murdered. "The ruler is trying for an eye-wash. He is highly diplomatic. But that's his job," said Sindhu.

Ridham's subject popped up occasionally and Sindhu detested it. He was worried. He had seen Ridham closely over the past days and felt that he was not reliable at all. Carnal desire ruled his life without scruples coming in the way.

Sindhu dined and left Koli's house late in the evening.

On his way back he stopped in front of a battered house. The house had been deserted for a long time. Creepers all over created a green veil over the burnt brick walls. Yet, it was a sprawling mansion with plenty of spacious rooms and a nice courtyard inside, more like Koli's house. The council had allotted this house to Sindhu. He would not stay in the cramped sack in the lower town anymore. But he could not relocate the next morning as he wished to. He had to wait a little as the house needed a major renovation.

The rainy season was close. Torrential downpour would start lashing the town any day now. The single-storeyed houses would be under water in a few days' time because the original platform was not high enough. A second floor needed to be built to be able to live in. This was generally done by filling up the whole of the single-story house with mud and debris to create an elevated solid base. This was generally done before the rain started.

Sindhu did not want to spend a single day more in the battered lower town. Standing there at the footstep of the mansion, Sindhu savoured losing himself in his dream. He imagined working on his artwork in a large hall facing the road. He would ask the artisans to provide plenty of windows in his rooms, unlike other houses. It should be airy. There must be moonlight flooding into the room at night. He shared everything with Koli but kept this to himself. It would be a surprise. This house was not very far from her place.

35

Ridham had paid several visits to Koli on the pretext of selling his fancy jewellery at throwaway prices. Koli showed all her acquisitions to Sindhu, who found the whole thing repulsive. He tried to convince Koli that the man might harbour evil intensions, but Koli dismissed them. Ridham was also being followed all the time by a bunch of spies appointed by the council, but Sindhu could not share this secret with Koli.

Finally, Sindhu decided to meet Ridham and broach the subject of concern.

Ridham was counting the day's earnings when Sindhu arrived at his little shed. The snake-charmer was seated on a dais against the wall waiting for his share of the day. A steady flame cast an orange glow over the walls.

Sindhu was offered a warm welcome.

They started to chat on the current market demand of various articles. Sindhu made aimless conversation, hoping that the snake charmer would leave after getting his share from Ridham. He did not want to broach the sensitive topic in front of the other man.

The snake charmer rose to his feet after the transaction was over. He was happy as the idea of a joint business had paid off well for him.

"Why don't you come to my place tomorrow? It's not far from here. I shall show you my recent acquisitions. You will love them!"

The snake charmer said, addressing Sindhu. He did not know the real reason behind their interest in his bundle of venomous snakes. He thought that Sindhu was simply curious about the reptiles.

Sindhu did not want to spoil this impression and asked, "Have you gotten some new snakes?"

"Yes I did. I found them beneath a pile of garbage behind this house. I swear, one bite and you will go to hell!"

Sindhu started to laugh looking at Ridham, "No. Not me. *He* will go to hell."

"Me?" Ridham smiled mischievously.

"Yes, you."

"As long as I get plenty to drink and enough women to sleep with, I don't care where I go!" Ridham said.

All three of them burst into boisterous laughter.

Sindhu assured the snake charmer, "I shall come and see your cute pets tomorrow morning."

"I have something to ask you." Sindhu said grimly, after the snake charmer had left.

Ridham stared curiously.

"Are you visiting Koli's house regularly?" Sindhu launched the question directly.

Suddenly Ridham was cross, "Yes, why do you ask?"

"I am concerned." Sindhu replied firmly.

"I visit that woman to sell my goods. What's wrong with that?" Ridham asked furtively.

"Are you sure?" Sindhu asked tersely.

"Do you suspect some other motive?"

"Yes I do, and I am not very comfortable with that. She happens to be the daughter of my mentor."

"Did you come here to dispense a holy sermon?"

"I told you that I feel responsible to ensure that the woman is safe."

"I am not a cannibal. I shall not eat her alive. I just go there to sell my goods. She is rich and can afford the kind of goods I sell."

"I am not sure of that. Ridham, I suggest you satiate your carnal desire somewhere else. Don't fix your eyes on her. She is a dignified lady."

Ridham started to laugh, "Now you have come to the point. I hate talking in riddles. Let me tell you I am not going to kill her, cheat her or rob her. I am only going to seduce her. Not forever, but only for a few days and then vanish for a very long time beyond the ocean. I have to embark on another voyage anyway. This will not damage her in any way. I am just trying to convince her about my good intentions. There is no harm on my agenda. She will be happy, I shall be happy. I think I am pretty close to my goal. A few days more and she will come running into my arms."

Sindhu listened quietly and fell silent for a long moment.

After some consideration, he said "Do you think you are on a safe road Ridham? I am your friend and hence am bothering to share a secret with you. You are a suspect in connection with Magan's death. If you get involved in another scandal, they will definitely not spare you. She happens to be the daughter of a very influential man who died not very long ago. If you mingle much with her, you risk your safety. Now, let me tell you one more thing. I am very well aware of what you have been selling her. She herself asked me to hand over this packet to you."

"What is this?"

"I don't know. I did not check, but she said that you have been selling things to her at absurd prices. She does not like the obligation. She said that this packet contains something to compensate your losses."

Ridham kept the packet aside. He wanted to check the contents later in privacy. He had himself observed that Koli was not very comfortable about accepting the goods he sold her at such low prices. That did not bother him. He just wanted her to understand the message. The packet was the assurance that the message was conveyed loud and clear. He would get another excuse to meet her now. Considering the prospects, he smiled slyly.

Sindhu noted the smile, "What made you smile?"

Ridham looked squarely at Sindhu and said, "I have a lot of plans you know."

"About what?"

"About how to savour the beauty. After all, I am going to be here just for few more days. I should be content when I leave, and she should realize that she has met a real man for the first time in her life!"

Sindhu stared at him in disgust. Finally he was ready to leave. He stopped for a moment at an afterthought and said, "Look, you will be doomed Ridham, if you pursue your nasty plan. I came to warn you. We have been friends. I wish that better sense prevails upon you."

Sindhu left in a huff.

36

Ridham donned a set of expensive clothes that he always kept neatly aside for special occasions. The night ahead was going to be special and long. The arrangements must be flawless. He must look impressive; a bit of rough maleness was also welcome. He combed his hair with great care. The hair must not be orderly yet not unkempt. He deliberated over a bath and decided against it. The idea of a sweaty tangle of flesh reeking of lusty passion appealed to him. He was prepared now. He considered taking the candle with him but finally discarded the idea. He knew the route like the back of his palm. Even if the torches by the side of the road had died out, he could tread through pitch darkness. A candle would make his movement unduly prominent. If guards were indeed watching him, darkness would be handy. Ridham closed the door and stepped onto the road.

Koli's message was clear. She did not leave an iota of doubt about her intent. She wanted Ridham to meet her at a house a few blocks away from her own at the stroke of midnight. She strictly forbade him from speaking to anyone. Surprises awaited him throughout the night Koli had assured in the letter. The message was explicit and straight. Ridham anticipated the flame of ravenous desire flaring up behind the gracious veneer of this dignified woman of society. The more he thought about her, the more he was overcome by the surge of lust.

Deeply immersed in his fantasy, he walked silently through the lanes and alleys. During the last few visits to her place, he had watched her minutely. Each of her movements seemed to pose a unique appeal to a man's eyes. Every flex of her slender waist, as she walked, twitched the root of carnal hunger... The expansive breasts swayed slightly, hinting at a throbbing pulse of passion. Ridham walked faster. He smiled impishly thinking about the savage ferocity with which he would plunder her impudent youth tonight. Koli apparently seemed to be brimming with pride all the time. Ridham resolved to tear her pride into pieces by imposing his ruthless domination. She would be brought to her knees begging for mercy when he would consume her subjugated womanhood.

Ridham found himself standing in front of the house Koli had asked him to wait at. Koli had clearly advised him to follow the signal of a candle. She would be waiting inside the abandoned house. As soon as Ridham appeared in front of the main gate, she would light the candle. Ridham was to simply follow the candle. This caution was necessary because Koli could not afford to risk her privacy in the society.

Ridham stood in front of the main gate and peered inside without stepping in. The door was ajar. The door did not have a latch because the house had been unoccupied for a very long time. After a few moments, there was a flicker of a faint yellow light near the door of a room that was located beyond the courtyard. Ridham swiftly stepped inside the house. The courtyard was full of various kinds of weeds and shrubs. He had to walk carefully without hurting his feet.

As soon as he entered the room, he could see the flame disappearing from the room. Koli held the candle and sauntered into another room through a doorway. Ridham saw her from behind. Her curvy profile was not apparent as she seemed to have covered herself with a robe from tip to toe. No one could have recognized her in that attire. Ridham followed her in a hurry. He planned to get rid of her robe patiently. The night was going to be long. He must cherish every moment of it. Koli's slender figure passed like an elusive shadow from one room to the other with Ridham following her in eagerness.

Suddenly she turned round the corner of a wall and disappeared. Ridham quickened his pace following the receding glow of light. Turning around the corner, Ridham encountered a flight of stairs leading down. He started to descend the stairs desperately. Koli was not in sight but her receding candle was lit his way by its faint glow. Finally Ridham found her standing inside a small enclosed cubicle surrounded by walls. She was trying to fix the candle on a little platform by the side of the wall with her back towards Ridham. Ridham appreciated the idea. This seemed to be a secret underground chamber. Nobody would even come here. The flame would also not go out as there was no wind. The thought of the entire act under the wavering flame of candle tantalized his senses.

He walked slowly into the confined space. As he approached Koli from behind, raging with a mad rush of desire, the flame suddenly went out and the blank void gulped Ridham in a blink. Something whooshed by creating a breeze and a thud sounded near him. Ridham panicked and called out, "Koli!"

There was no response. He stepped ahead trying to feel for her without stretched hands. But after a few steps he hit the wall. He traced the surface and suddenly the molten wax scorched his skin. He shrieked. Solid silence was jammed inside the space seamlessly. He called out again, "Koli?"

Nobody answered. He realized that he was probably alone here; Koli had left. He walked back, trying to guess the route, but the darkness destroyed his sense of direction. After a few attempts struggling in all directions, Ridham found a door that was locked from outside. The thud he had heard was that of the shutting door. Fear gripped his consciousness. He screamed with all his might, "Koli!" There was not even an echo. His own voice greeted him in cold mockery.

Suddenly he heard a sound above his head and looked up, but he could not make out anything in the darkness. Feeble sounds of something heavy being dragged, reached his ears. He was alert. In a moment the glow of a candle returned faintly, but from the cracks in the boards in the ceiling above his head. The ceiling seemed to be opening up with a crack. Ridham was relieved and looked up. Suddenly the roof opened up and there was light for a brief moment. Ridham screamed again, "Koli!"

Before he could grasp what was over his head, darkness tumbled back at a rapid pace. Something black was trying to block the opening in the roof. In a moment, the entire opening was almost blocked and a huge block of stone toppled over the edge of the opening. Ridham felt the monstrous load crushing him to death in savage vengeance. He tried to scream but could not. Darkness gobbled him.

After a few moments, the roof opened again and a heap of garbage poured through the gap. The confined space was quickly filled with a huge stone, the body of a man with a smashed head and a dump of rubbish. As soon as it was full, the roof was placed back in its place.

The candle was snuffed out in the room upstairs.

37

The heavy wooden door swung open and the ruler barged in. The head priest was startled faintly. No one ever dared to invade his privacy in such a brazen manner in the past, not even the ruler. He looked at the ruler questioningly with an irritated frown.

"Are you behind this atrocity?" demanded the ruler. His voice trembled with fury.

"What are you talking about?" said the priest with unwavering calmness.

"You know very well. I want a straight answer." The ruler held him under his frozen stare.

"I don't like people talking in riddles with me. Come to the point or get lost. Don't waste my time," The priest snapped.

"One man disappeared. The other died a terrible death. A bundle of venomous snakes were let loose in his room in the middle of the night! It is a typical method of ancient sacrifice!"

"Ah! I see. Let me be very clear to you. Sacrifice is the best solution to ward off the impending peril. If some wise men are performing human sacrifice, the civilization would be saved from being vanquished. What are you complaining about?"

"There is no peril looming large. We are absolutely safe. It is you who is creating the unnecessary panic. Moreover, I had strictly banned any kind of sacrifice long back. It seems to have starting to raise its ugly head once again. I want to know if you are the master mind."

"I shall not answer your stupid question. I support such action. I am not a fool like you. I have the responsibility to save the community. And sacrifice is the only way."

"So…it's you!"

"I don't care what you think. Let me warn you…never again question me like that; or else you will indeed face serious consequences. For old time's sake, I pardon you once…"

38

"You are being appointed as the head of the secret community, the torch bearer of the legacy of our empire to lead us to a glorious future." The ruler welcomed Sindhu majestically to join the elite group of officials of the council.

Sindhu went up the dais and received the burnt clay tablet engraved with the stamp of authorization and approval. He had earned it by his sincere and dedicated work over a long period of time.

The heads of all the councils from the various towns had gathered for the conclave. They welcomed Sindhu in his new role. His reputation as an artist of deep thought and intellect had spread across the land. His standing was beyond question.

His duty now, was to propagate the central theme behind the backbone of the empire over the crème of the younger generation. The secret community would be guided by him. They would learn the background of the conventions. They would learn to respect them and ensure the continuity of the traditions into the future.

Sindhu enjoyed his work. The respect and fame served his ambition well. This was what he had always aspired for. The younger generation loved his company. They were mesmerized when he spoke. Though at times, the basic question popped up in his mind, "Is it worth saving all these conventions and practices?" Yet he kept this disturbing thought at the back of his mind. He, being an artist, had at one time hated this infallible repetition and regularity. Today he preached the same. But, there was no other way. To keep his position and station in society, he must conceal his radical thinking.

When he visited Koli's place some evenings, this aspect was often broached by Koli. She argued savagely that there was a conflict between what Sindhu thought and what he spoke. The discussion fed their intellectual hunger and nothing more. Finally, Sindhu accepted that he did this for living.

Koli often asked about Ridham, "Where did he disappear overnight?"

This question bothered both of them and they ended up in a stretch of speculation for hours together. Finally, they always wound up at a conclusion: Ridham had simply left for another voyage, though neither of them was sure about it.

Yet, Sindhu never gave up, but came back to the question in a roundabout manner, "He had designs on you. I am sure his intention was not mere friendship, but much more."

Koli laughed it away, "Come on! He never even hinted at any such evil thing. I am not as cheap as you think. I would have taken him to task in that case. He was just trying to sell some expensive stuff to me. He thought I could afford them."

"Don't misunderstand me. I don't ever dare to think that you are cheap. I mean, Ridham thought ill of you. Whether you accept it or not, you know it well," Sindhu argued. He was not convinced.

Life sailed by in an eventless rhythm.

There was peace and silence. Sindhu remained in regular contact with Koli. Koli enjoyed her solitude, yet the occasional discourse with Sindhu filled her silent evenings with verve for life.

Koli sometimes thought about Girad and his imminent return. But that day was far away. Girad's absence brought comfort to her. They had never enjoyed each other's company anyway.

The ruler called Sindhu one morning.

"The council has decided to set up a separate house for the secret community. Lately, the bath house is becoming extremely crowded with various sorts of people frequenting it morning, noon and night. The serenity of the house is spoiled. I don't think that you can conduct your lectures there. Moreover, disturbing developments are being reported from various part of the empire. Groups of nomads have entered our land. They have come from beyond the mountain in the northwest. Their arrival has been very silent and nobody noticed in the beginning. Now, it has been reported that they are starting to flex their muscles to overpower our people. I am planning to set up an army already. What worries me more is their attempt to absorb our citizens into their faith and belief. In one settlement, when they could not impose their pantheon of gods on our men and women, they seemed to have started worshipping our God of fertility."

Sindhu could not follow, "You mean that the nomads are worshipping our God of fertility?"

"Yes, you are right. You know, our people are innocent and gullible. They seem to be influenced by the fake show of open mindedness by these nomads. The strict adherence to our culture has been compromised. There is a give and take. Finally, the nomads are getting a toe hold on our land. I can't let this happen. We must be able to hold our fort with grit and resolve. Your secret community will play an extremely critical role in this."

Sindhu was thrilled at the prospect of an independent office.

"I have decided to build a new building with a courtyard and several classrooms for you. In the courtyard, I plan to install a statue. This statue should also convey the central theme of your mission - the mission of the secret community. It should also exude the mixed expression of secrecy, power, enigma and so on. You have to work on the sculpture."

Sindhu asked, "Shall I do it in bronze?"

"No. I got a block of black stone gifted by one of the lords of some faraway land. This kind of stone is not found here. I shall send that block to your place right away. You will sculpt a beautiful statue out of it. This will be your masterpiece, Sindhu."

Sindhu went back with his heart skipping in excitement. This statue would immortalize him. It was more than what he expected in life.

The same evening, he could not help but land up at Koli's door.

"Do you know what I am going to tell you?"

"No. I don't know at all," Koli laughed.

"I have been commissioned to create a sculpture by the council. This statue will be a legendary work of mine."

He narrated the entire story to her. Koli shared his excitement and they explored various ideas to represent the image desired by the council.

Suddenly, in the middle of the discussion, Sindhu was distracted. Koli did not notice for a while but then asked, "You are lost somewhere."

Sindhu stared at her absently.

Koli was perplexed, "What is the matter?"

With a sudden start, Sindhu rose to his feet and prepared to leave.

"Hey…where are you going?" asked Koli, totally puzzled.

Sindhu almost ran out of the house. Just before disappearing, he said, "I have gotten the right idea. I am going to start right now!"

BOOK III

39

"Open all the packages." The guard commanded.

"I already have." Girad replied smugly.

"You seem to have come back rather early!" observed the head of the customs guard inspecting the stamped seal.

Girad smiled, "You are right. I felt homesick."

The guard ran his sceptical eyes over the various packages of goods sprawled in front of him. "Don't bluff, we know you well. You must have made a fortune very quickly; perhaps swindled someone down there beyond the ocean. It was better for you to run away."

Girad burst into boisterous laughter.

"Why the hell are you laughing?" The guard snapped.

"You can clearly see what I have come back with. Everything is in front of you: just a few bags of dry fruits, some bits of jewels that we don't find in this land, some more simple stuff and a statue of black stone. Is it a fortune?" Girad asked playfully.

The guards remained silent gazing at the articles for a long moment, and finally gave up. "Well… we don't see much. Let us calculate the requisite tax for the council now."

The tax was calculated and charged. Girad shared some of the articles that he had brought in. Shortly, he was on his way home.

"Who is it?" Koli was busy dusting the house when there was a knock on the door.

"It's me!" Girad announced.

Koli was taken aback and reacted reflexively, "You!"

She forced a smile, but the flitting expression of shock failed to hide her bitterness.

"You are upset, huh!" Remarked Girad caustically.

Koli imposed an artificial excitement in her behaviour and tried to overshadow her misgivings.

After resting for a short while, Girad settled with the goods that he had brought. Koli was not interested in his merchandise and involved herself in some household chores.

40

It had been raining cats and dogs for the past several days. The river started to swell alarmingly. The elevated platform that cradled the settlement was arrogantly challenged once again. It had happened so many times in the past. As soon as the scar of the earlier cataclysm was effaced from the mind of the inhabitants, a new cloud of disaster gathered on the horizon.

Several lanes were already clogged with water. Some mud houses had collapsed here and there. The homeless population was increasing in number.

Koli stood by the window and watched the rain drops rushing down from the sky. The drops were fairly larger in size than usual. She loved the rains, but the ferocity of the downpour felt ominous. The news of the swelling river sent a feeling nervous apprehension to every soul in the town. Often the surging waves craned their haughty heads over the edge of the platform.

Koli was startled by a heavy thud at the door. The rude knocking did not stop. The guest seemed to be desperate to enter the house. Irritated and curious, Koli rushed to open the door.

"We come from the customs department of the council. Is Girad there?" demanded an official. In a state of shock, Koli observed almost a dozen guards peering over her shoulder into the house. She did not like the hostile aura of their mood.

"He is not at home," Koli replied curtly.

"Well, we have to still search your house. The council feels that he has not declared all the goods that he had brought in through the border." announced the head of the team.

Koli considered the possibility. She knew it was obvious. Girad could not be transparent and honest. Neither did she feel any concern for his safety.

"You can have a look." She stepped aside to let them in.

For a reasonable span of time, the customs officials surveyed every inch of the house and finally concluded that there was a slight error in his declaration.

"We must adjust this slight difference by taking an article from his collection. I leave this to you madam. You decide what we should carry with us."

Koli went into the room where Girad had piled all his stuff. After running her eyes for a brief moment, she fixed them on a black statue.

She deliberated for a while. Out of all the goods, an object of art would be of least concern to Girad. She made up her mind, and picked up the statue. It was quite heavy. She took a quick look at it and admired the work.

"You can take this," Koli handed over the artifact to them and they left.

After a while, Girad rushed into the house in panic. He was totally drenched from head to toe. "Did anyone from the customs come here?" He demanded nervously.

Koli nodded.

"What did they take with them?"

"Oh! They found a slight difference between your declaration and your actual goods. I gave them a black stone statue." Koli replied in a self-assured manner.

"What?" Girad was crestfallen.

"Why? It was just a statue. I thought you did not admire such things much, so I gave it to them. I thought that the other items seemed to be of your choice."

Girad crashed onto the ground in despair. "You are a fool! Why did you have to do that? You idiot!"

Koli flinched in disgust, "That's why I wasn't happy when you came back. Listen, I don't want any part of your treachery; understood?"

Girad glared at her for a moment and left the house in a huff.

It was no use arguing with Koli, the damage was already done. He had purchased the black statue with a purpose. He had managed to scoop out all the stone from inside and made it hollow with a cap to block the bottom. The statue was filled with precious stones and jewels. The customs could never have detected the catch. Now, that Koli had given it to the council, the very purpose of his arduous trip to the faraway land had been defeated.

While contriving a plan to get the statue back, he rushed towards the council.

At the council, the ruler was discussing various aspects of the secret community with Sindhu.

"By the way, how far has the sculpture progressed? How long will it take to complete?" asked the ruler.

Sindhu feared this question the most. In a fit of passion, he had made a blunder one evening. He must find a way to get around the disaster. For quite some time now, the ruler had been asking about the statue, but Sindhu somehow managed to evade a firm answer; because, he had none.

Today, his eyes suddenly caught the black stone statue resting on the ground next to the ruler's pedestal. From the corner of his eyes, he watched the shiny black thing and became confident that the stone was no different from what had been assigned to him. An idea flashed in his mind.

"That is a nice piece of craft," Sindhu mentioned casually.

"Yes. It is made of the same stone as the one you are working on. The guards have confiscated it from Girad's house this morning."

Sindhu was shocked, "What? Do you mean that Girad has come back already?"

The ruler nodded his head regretfully, "Yes. He returned only a few days ago."

"But... but, I thought some emissary was deputed to Dilmun to bring back the cylindrical seal, and Girad was supposed to be persuaded to stay back... perhaps forever..."

"Yes, that was the plan. We had dispatched the emissary also, but this character left Dilmun before the emissary could reach him!"

Sindhu absorbed the disappointment. An idea flashed in his mind. He could escape the sculpture problem. He went close to the black statue and ran his hand over its shining surface. "You see, the nature of this art is quite different than that of ours. I always dreamed of owning a statue like this."

The ruler smiled, "You like that so much?"

"Yes, I do. In fact, I can study the nature of their art if I get a sample like this."

"You can take it, if you want," the ruler declared.

"But while studying it, it might be damaged. I shall scrape the surface and check the properties of the material. This will save the block you have given me."

"It is yours. Do whatever you want with it."

Sindhu did not waste any more time and left the council with the statue immediately lest the ruler changed his mind.

Girad earnestly urged the official, "Look, I need it back only for a brief period. I promise to come and personally hand over the statue to the council. Believe me."

"Why do you need it back so dearly?" The official looked at him in grave suspicion.

"Because I had bought it for a close friend of mine who admires art. You people have taken it away. I want to at least show him that I had actually got it for him. Since, the council has confiscated the statue I cannot present it to him anymore. Otherwise he will think that I had simply bluffed about it to him. It will spoil our relationship. Please…" Girad was on his knees.

The official considered the reliability of what was told. It sounded almost convincing. "But the statue is with the ruler. He kept it in his chamber. You have to meet the ruler in order to get it back. We cannot take up such a strange proposal for you."

After some time, Girad was standing in front of the ruler.

"What? The statue?"

"Just for a brief period of time. I shall myself bring it back before sunset. I promise."

"But, our master designer had just taken it with him."

"Who is that? Sindhu?"

"Yes, do you know him?"

In an instant, Girad was out of the chamber again. He sprinted along the lanes in manic despondence.

41

After Girad had left the house in desperation, Koli remained stupefied for a long moment. She wondered about the cause of his attachment to the sculpture. It was incredible that during his sojourn, he had developed a fancy for art. His continued rowdy behaviour showed that he had not changed a bit. Then what had made the statue so dear to him?

The statue was indeed beautiful. Koli tried to think of the sculpture once more. There was something special about it, but she could not place her finger on it. Nevertheless, it could not attract any extraordinary commercial value in her view. Then what was it that made it precious to Girad? Nothing ever appealed to him other than the price.

Having passed the statue to the guards, a slight pinch of guilt nagged at the back of her mind. If possible, she would get another one like that from the market. But, the question hung like a large question mark. What lay hidden beneath its shining black exterior? After fretting over it for a long moment, she decided that the only person who could help her was Sindhu.

Immediately, she started for Sindhu's place, which was not far from her home. Sindhu had never invited her home, but she knew where he lived. It was a large mansion in the upper town. The council had offered it to him after he had occupied the post of Master Designer of the council.

Koli hurried along the muddy lane, covering her head with a piece of thick cloth to avoid getting completely drenched. Nevertheless, the ferocious splatter of rain soaked her immediately. It was difficult to step forward because the sheet of rain formed an opaque wall in front of her. She trembled internally. From within her house, she had not known the severity of the situation. Finally she arrived at Sindhu's door.

Koli knocked softly on the door.

After a brief silence, the door opened slightly and Sindhu peered through the crack. He blinked in disbelief and then asked tentatively, "Is everything okay?"

"Not really. I want some advice from you." Koli said.

"About what?"

Koli was now exasperated, "I can't speak like this standing outside your house. Will you not ask me to come inside?"

Sindhu did not move but stayed hidden behind the slightly ajar door with his head sticking through the gap.

"Come on, what is bothering you? I want to enter. I must discuss something with you urgently. Moreover, it's raining heavily outside," Koli insisted impatiently.

A faint cryptic smile flitted across Sindhu's lips, "Well, I thought, maybe another day…"

"I don't understand! You are behaving strangely!" Koli was puzzled.

"I mean, it could have been another day. Nevertheless, it does not matter. Let it be today. Welcome home!" Sindhu smiled broadly and opened the door and Koli stepped inside.

She had never seen his home but always imagined how Sindhu lived. Sindhu remained near the door, while Koli ran her curious eyes around the room. It was a richly furnished living room decorated with exotic objects of art. The burnt brick walls had also been painted by Sindhu. The walls were decorated with images of wild bushes and dense foliage. She felt as if she was standing in the middle of a forest.

Koli gasped in fascination. Sindhu watched her silently with a twinkle in his eyes.

Suddenly, her captivated spell stumbled onto something eerie. She was instantly alert and looked again to confirm if it was an illusion. No, it was real!

"The statue!" she murmured.

Sindhu laughed softly, "Yes. I am sure it is the same statue. You did not expect it here, I know. That's why I was hesitating to let you enter. But, life runs in one direction only. We can never roll back our moments. By the way, there are more surprises in store for you, my friend."

Koli stared at Sindhu with her eyes wide in shock, "How did it find its way here?"

"I asked, and the ruler let me take it. Simple!" Sindhu said nonchalantly.

"But why?" Koli demanded.

Sindhu paced across the room with a faint smile on his lips. After a few moments, he looked at her squarely and said with a sense of finality, "That's a long story. Come into my studio. You should know everything. You have chosen the time, not me. You must take it all, right today. Come…" He clutched the statue and entered the passage that led out from the living room. Koli followed almost in a hypnotic trance. The passage had a few rooms on both sides. Finally, Sindhu gestured to Koli to follow him into his studio.

Once inside, Sindhu indicated to her to stand in the centre of the hall. He went to another sculpture that was covered with a veil of cloth. Koli watched in anticipation while Sindhu removed the veil resting mysteriously over the sculpture.

Koli shrieked in shock. Quickly, her confounded countenance transformed into a blush. She quivered in mortification, yet could not turn her gaze away from what stood in front of her eyes; an exquisite statue carved from the same black stone depicting Koli in the nude. Her full bloomed bearing, in a seductively inviting posture framed by a doorway, looked straight with wide open eyes, gleaming with sparkles of mischief. The blooming fullness of the breasts heaved in passion; the perilous curves lured the onlooker in shameless arrogance. Everything about the sculpture appeared perversely alive. A stunned silence fell like a thunder. Neither of them spoke. Koli stared at the statue, astounded. Countless questions jostled against each other for priority. Yet, she failed to focus on any of them.

She never noticed Sindhu receding from her view. Koli was suddenly startled to consciousness when she felt Sindhu's presence right behind her. He whispered into her ears while putting on a necklace of bright carnelian beads around her slender neck, "You know what? I have loved you all this while, only the words floundered. I was waiting for this day for a lifetime. I made this necklace for you. I made love to you in my dreams each time I stuck a bead into this necklace. How beautiful you look in this! You are my dream; my eternal love." Koli shivered but could not move, as if rooted to the spot by an unseen dictate. Sindhu embraced her and kissed her in feverish longing. Koli's moralistic prohibitions collapsed like a house of cards under the savage onslaught of her everlasting longing for the man she loved. She was swept away by the deluge of passion for the man that she had desired for so long. Sindhu's voracious mouth plundered her treasured sweetness for an eternity. After what seemed like a lifetime of sailing over the waves of passion, Koli drifted back to consciousness. Mustering all her strength, she shoved him away. Sindhu almost fell to the ground but somehow managed to stay on his feet.

Koli's compelling resistance awakened him from his stupor of obsessive trance. He composed himself.

"You have always been my desire Koli. You were also in love with me, weren't you? You wanted me, not that savage monster."

Koli spoke, still dazed with what had transpired a moment ago, "Of course, I had wanted you! But you never spelt out your willingness to be with me. When father had proposed our alliance, you shied away. Why did you do that? Why did you hide your feelings for such a long time? Today, when half of our lives are lost, you are divulging your feelings at last; that too in a creepy manner! Girad has come back now. What do you intend to do?"

"I was planning to tell you about my feelings, but the idiot came back too early. He was not supposed to come back at all. Anyway, his return is a blessing in disguise for me. Look at that statue. You know what?"

Koli stared at him inquisitively.

"The ruler told me to carve a statue for the secret community. It is supposed to be installed at the courtyard of the new building where we shall teach the students. Do you remember that we had discussed it one evening?. The structure must convey enigma, mystery and beauty. The first image that flashed in my mind was this. Your body was the embodiment of all those impressions. Your existence meant an unfathomable depth of fog. You could be explored for a lifetime yet the depth would remain beyond reach. In a fit of passion, I grabbed that dark block of stone and started to carve your statue. At some point, I realized that this image might not be welcomed by the council. You are known to the members. As soon as they would cast their eyes on it, they would know it was your figure. This would be deemed to be a perverse sacrilege. I could not afford to expose it to the ruler, but this stone is rare in this land. Thanks to the fool I could get another lump of black-stone. Luckily, the customs had confiscated it from your house. The ruler let me take it. I shall now keep this sculpture of yours in my private custody and modify the other statue for the council. But you see, the sculpture I made from the dead block of stone is almost as sensuous as you are."

Koli listened in stunned silence and demanded bluntly, "Why did you decline father's proposal that day? Was there really a girl you loved?"

"No, I cooked up that story. I was forced to do so, because your man tricked me into believing that he was a special advisor of the council, and if I did not convince your father to hand you over to him, he would spoil my prospects of getting a job as an artist! Moreover, he framed me as a thief who had stolen his identity seal. He had simply planted the seal in my pocket when I was leaving the council." Sindhu spoke in exasperation.

Koli muttered spitefully, "You mean that you brought him to us to accomplish your own agenda? How could you be so callous?"

"Callous! Do you remember that face peeking in through your window that night?"

"Yes of course! How is that relevant?"

"That was your Girad. Still you call me callous!" Sindhu cried out in desperation.

Koli flinched away in disgust. "Knowing everything, you urged me to destroy my life, just because of your own selfish interests. You are as treacherous as Girad! How can you claim that you ever loved me?"

"You call me treacherous! You have no idea about what I have done just to keep you safe all the time. I never let another man cast his evil eyes on you. Without my protection, you would be nowhere, with your precious chastity. How can you disregard my resolute commitment?"

Sindhu spoke fervently possessed by delirious vehemence.

Koli was intrigued, "What have you done?"

"Good question. Then listen." Sindhu took a deep breath and resumed his dialogue, "Do you think that idiot of yours had the luck to win the gamble against Ridham?"

Sindhu stared at Koli in cynical mockery for a few moments and then fed the answer himself, "No! He could only lose. Such was his skill and luck. But, what happened that night? Have you ever wondered what brought him that reed boat?"

Koli remained silent.

"I got him that damn boat!" Sindhu announced.

Koli was at a loss, "But why?"

"Because I wanted him to leave you alone. I knew he was desperate to go on a voyage beyond the ocean, and a reed boat was essential for that. I made countless invaluable objects of art for Ridham in exchange for that reed boat. I struck a bargain with Ridham that he should lose his boat in a gamble to Girad. It worked well. You see, nobody had a clue!"

Koli was still unable to connect all the pieces of the puzzle.

Sindhu went on, "The ruler hated Girad for his dubious background. He detested your man even more when he mounted a bargain with the council. He wanted the subsidy for a voyage in exchange for the seal. Then a secret advisor came forward and convinced the ruler that it would be wise to send Girad overseas with the new cylindrical seal. The mastermind of the thieves himself would be the custodian of the new seal. The ruler was convinced and sanctioned the subsidy. The council even organized to send an emissary to ensure that he never came back, but settled there forever. The idiot left too early, before the emissary could reach him with his message. Do you know who that secret advisor was?"

Koli murmured, "You...!"

"You are correct. So, this dirty chap left at last one evening and I felt relieved. But another nuisance emerged from nowhere; that buffoon called Magan." Sindhu seemed to lapse into abstraction for a moment.

"Magan! Do you mean...?" mumbled Koli in anticipation.

"Who knows why that innocent young man had to fall in love with you? He was blind. I warned him on countless occasions. I tried to persuade him to forget you; but he would not listen. He even gifted you that bloody necklace!" Sindhu ruminated in retrospect.

After a few quick breaths, Sindhu spoke again. "During the festival, he was smitten by your beauty. When I was sure that he would not listen to me, I had to carry out my duty."

"What do you mean?" Koli's voice trembled.

"I killed him. I know how to deal with snakes better than the snake charmer. There were plenty of snakes in the port town where I grew up. I could live in a house with a dozen lethal snakes. I slipped into Magan's room as soon as Ridham left in the middle of the night. I simply let the most venomous of the reptiles loose around his drunken face. They did the job."

Koli turned her face away in fear and disgust.

"Listen, that's not all. This earth is full of dirt! The filthy merchant called Ridham, whom you took to be almost a saint, was actually desperate to ravish your body. He just wanted to sleep with you. Everything else was pretext."

Koli watched him with a frown from the corner of her eyes.

"He died too. You see, I sent him a fake invitation for a rendezvous from you. At that time the council had just allotted this mansion to me. It was a deserted house, full of debris. I coaxed him to come here in the thick of the night and led him into an underground storeroom, right below where you are standing now. The idiot mistook me for you because I had put on a flowing cloak to mislead him. I simply pushed a massive rock over the edge of the roof. It smashed his filthy head and took his breath away."

Koli stared at him in utter disbelief and repulsion. "And the entire town mistook it for sacrifice!" Koli mumbled.

Sindhu started to laugh hysterically, "Yes! That too was my ploy. The day that stupid priest announced the prophecy; I encountered a few men talking about sacrifice in the inn. I went back to the inn few days later to employ them as my tools. They fell for my trap. I disguised myself as an old man and they thought that I was a messenger from the priest. I made them carry out a few animal sacrifices in a spectacular manner. Soon words took flight and the entire town was abuzz with the talk of sacrifice of animals as per the ancient rituals. My plan was to trick Girad into a trap of sacrifice…I mean, to get him killed in the guise of human sacrifice. But, before that, I managed to send him out of the town itself and he sailed across the ocean. I spared his life, but today I repent for doing so. Anyhow, my scheme of ritualistic sacrifice paid off and those other two fools are now dead! I am anyway glad for the adamant stand of the senile priest. The ruler consulted even with me about the alleged sacrifice. He believed that the old man was responsible for the whole thing. When asked, the idiot god-man never denied the charge just because of his ego!"

For a while, silence reigned heavy in the air between them. Sindhu seemed to be lost in some reverie with a faint smile of satisfaction on his lips.

"You know what? When I discovered that Girad had no connection with the council, and had cheated me, I confronted him. I still cannot forget his derisive laughter. He told me that he did not care to put on a mask any more. He had gotten you in his bed, and that was all he wanted; He did not care about what I thought of him. I had warned him that afternoon that the game would not be over until I took something back from him. And I am taking it back; it is you who I shall take back, today!"

Koli stood riveted to the spot trying to swallow the shocking revelations.

Sindhu spoke as an afterthought, "You asked what I have done for you! Do you remember the seal that you had lost on your way back home from the council some time back? You were carrying two heavy sacks full of articles disbursed by the council."

Koli blinked in anticipation but never said a word. Many events shrouded in mystery were unfolding one by one. She could not follow the working of Sindhu's mind.

Sindhu added, "I carried it to your home, and that's why in the morning you found it at your doorstep. I followed you most of the time whenever you travelled alone. No shadow of distress could touch your skin. I was always there. I even sent you a set of burnt clay jewellery before the festival. But, you made the mistake of applying that stupid red pigment on your head. You looked ravishing but you seemed to belong to that scum. I could not stand to see you that way. You never applied any of that red pigment before, which suited me well. Only I have the right to apply that pigment on your head. You belong to me alone. That's why that morning, I drew your attention to the back of the house for a moment and smashed the ornaments before you got back. Such is my passion for you! I cannot compromise on my love. Anything that comes in my way must perish! Understood?"

Suddenly, Sindhu grabbed Koli and subjugated her tremulous figure forcibly. Koli tried to resist, but the shock had numbed her senses. Sindhu ravaged every part of her physical existence in manic lust. She lay there obeying his savage dictates. Koli was oblivious to the passage of time, and let herself feed Sindhu's eternal hunger. He groaned that she had always been his woman. She must compensate for his loss of half a life of sacrifice. She must undergo the grind of his ruthless passion trapped for eternity.

Suddenly there were footsteps in the house. Someone had barged into the mansion in a desperate fit. The sound penetrated feebly into Sindhu's consciousness, and he lifted his eyes to see who had intruded into his house.

Girad's stocky figure stood in the doorway. He glowered at the two bodies locked in a passionate embrace.

"What is going on?" Girad bellowed fiercely.

Sindhu rose to his feet and replied with unfazed calmness, "You can see for yourself. Let me clarify that I am simply taking back what you had stolen from me long ago."

"I see. I always suspected that you wanted to sleep with that woman. You are no different from me. I don't care much. I have slept enough with that snobbish bitch. You can take her now. But I can promise that you will find her stale after a few days. I came here for something else but not that bloody bitch."

Sindhu stared at him apprehensively.

Girad pointed at the black statue that he had brought from overseas. "I want that back in exchange for this woman. It sounds like a good bargain to me, what do you say? Keep her as long as you like."

Sindhu shook his head in denial, "You are mistaken. I have always loved her. There is no point explaining such matters to a morbid rascal like you. Listen, I shall never give you back that statue. You can forget about it."

Girad weighed Sindhu's words for a moment, and then sounded a calm warning, "Well, I request you to hand it over to me once more. Will you return the black statue to me?"

"No!"

In a sudden move, Girad dashed and reached behind Sindhu. He grabbed Koli's sculpture. As Sindhu had been guarding the sculpture, Girad had no idea that there were two statues in the room. As he lifted the wrong one, Sindhu shrieked in fear, "Put that down right now!"

Girad looked at the object he held in his hand, and realized his mistake. He did not move but swayed it in the air.

Sindhu trembled in anxiety, fearing that the dearest thing in the world might be destroyed. An idea flashed in his head, and he lifted the other statue suddenly.

"Let us exchange," suggested Girad playfully.

"Forget it. If that sculpture is damaged in any way, I shall smash yours into small bits," warned Sindhu.

They rested their alert eyes on one another and moved around in a circle. Meanwhile, Koli fumbled for her tattered clothes and wrapped them around her body. She managed to stand on her feet, though she felt uncertain and dazed. It took a while for her to realize the scene unfolding in front of her eyes. She screamed hoarsely in unspeakable agony, "Both of you are sick! I hate your very shadows! Go to hell and take your statues with you; and never try to come near me again! I shall kill you!"

Before they could react, Koli rushed out of the room.

Sindhu yelled, "Where are you going?"

Koli's receding voice wafted back, "I am going to the council."

"Koli!" Both men shouted in desperation.

Instantly, they started to chase her. They caught up with Koli at the exit of the mansion.

Suddenly a muted gargling sound mingled with wild screams drew their attention. As they looked at the road, they found a huge mob running in frenzy, as if running for their lives. Sindhu and Girad craned their heads to see what had driven the mass crazy. One glimpse and they froze in fear. The river had jumped over the platform and was rushing in mad fury. The raging wave was hurtling down the lane swiping everything on its way. It was a deluge. The prophecy had turned true. The catastrophe had arrived indeed.. It was not clear from the distance if the mob was running ahead of it for life or they were being carried by the surge. The fearful screams grew louder but made no comprehensible meaning to the tree terrified human beings. In drunken fury, the stream of water carried death on its cradle.

Koli, Girad and Sindhu knew that they could not escape; the walls of the mansion were too weak to withstand the blow. They joined the mob and ran breathlessly.

They passed by the broader lanes of the upper town and landed in the dingy alleys of the suburb. Looking back was not an option. The cataclysm was chasing them with unwavering grit.

As they rushed through the narrow track between the rows of quarters for the menial workers, Sindhu stumbled into something and the statue slipped from his hand. The shinning black sculpture hit the ground with a crushing blow. A myriad of sparkling jewels sprang out like sparks of flying colors. Girad shrieked but could not stop to collect the scattering gems. Sindhu groaned in pain as he collapsed onto the ground. Koli slowed for a moment to look back.

The apocalypse chased them in manic ferocity. Terrorstruck, Sindhu watched as the giant wave approached him and finally gulped him into its dense strangling womb. In a blink, he was lifted off the ground and swept away. Water rushed in through his mouth and nose. He made a last foiled attempt to clutch something by his flailing hands but there was nothing but water.

Girad was fast losing his breath. His legs seemed to refuse the dictate of brain. Koli saw Sindhu being swallowed up by the wave and knew the inevitability. She stopped and let the flood embrace her earthly existence. The dynasty, the millennium old empire, its grand legacy were collapsing into a heap of debris.

In a few moments, all of them were blown away along with their love, lust and passion; as if they never existed on the face of the earth.

BACK TO THE RUINS...THREE MILLENNIA LATER...

The curious trowel scooped up a lump of grey soil from the ravaged earth. Instantly, three pairs of eager eyes were arrested by the bright and colourful sparkles dotting the pale mass of dust and clay. Several fingers approached the glittering riot of sparkles with tentative anticipation. They picked out the source of the sparkles: stones — semiprecious and precious!

"What brought them here?" The chief archaeologist mumbled.

"It is the most unusual abode for these gems! These appear as old as the soil," observed his assistant.

"These barracks must be the lodgings for the lowest class of the society." The chief raised his eyes distantly.

"You are right. We already found large mansions in the upper town."

"Then how could they land here?"

The thief was watching them curiously all the time. The excitement of the archaeologists fascinated him more than the unearthed jewels. He let out his unsolicited comment, "Maybe it is the hoard of a thief; poor chap could never use the stuff but only stashed it under the heap of garbage; fool!"

One of them turned his eyes absently, "No. These are scattered all over the place. Someone purposefully threw away the treasure he had."

"Why might one do so?"

"We shall never know. The legends of passion and greed always vanish with dried tears and faded laughter. What remains are a pile of lifeless bricks and stones."

ABOUT THE NOVEL

This novel is set against the backdrop of the declining phase of Indus-Saraswati Civilization. The civilization had vanished leaving behind some meticulously planned deserted towns such as Mohenjo-Daro, Harappa or Lothal, to name a few.

The events in the novel take place in the town of Mohenjo-Daro. The meaning of the word in local parlance was the mound of dead. I have avoided the speculative name, Meluha, that appeared in Mesopotamian texts. It is yet to ascertain if the word, Meluha, referred to Indian subcontinent. One can only be sure that Meluha was located outside the Persian Gulf.

While the plot and the characters are my imagination, the facts about the civilization depicted in the novel are based on authentic archaeological findings. For instance, the game of dice was popular among the people those days. Several dice had been recovered from the remains. Carnelian beads were used in ornaments. The archaeological finds have plenty of original as well as fake carnelian beads. Fossils of sea fishes were found all over the settlements. Some of the settlements were not even close to any river. Hence it is natural to conclude that people ate dried fish those days. Several terracotta models of bullock-cart bear testimony to their mode of transport over land. Hence all such details have been used to present a vivid picture of life in Mohenjo-Daro.

Of course, the prevailing counting system is not known to us yet. Hence it is not possible to describe numbers the way they did. I have taken the liberty of using the modern terminology to describe numbers in the book. The reader has to consider that the characters in the book used their native words for the relevant numbers.

The disappearance of the legendary civilization is shrouded with mystery. There are several possibilities. Flood was the most likely cause. The past will reveal itself one day and we shall see what made it vanish off the face of the earth.

BIBLIOGRAPHY

Thapar Romila. *The Penguin History of Early India*. Penguin India, Delhi.

L. Possehl Gregory. *The Indian Civilization, A contemporary Perspective*. Vistaar Publications.

Levi Sylvain, Jean Przyluski and Jules Bloch. *Pre-Aryan and Pre-Dravidian in India*. Asian Educational Services.

Dilip K. Chakrabarty. The *Oxford Companion to Indian Archeology*.

Abraham Eraly. Gem in the Lotus. Penguin Books.

John Keay. India: a History, Harper Perennial.

Upinder Singh. A History of Ancient and Medieval India. Pearson.

D.P.Agrawal. Harappan technology and its legacy. RUPA.

Wendy Doniger. The Hindus, An alternative history. Penguin Viking.

Barret, D. An Early India Toy. Oriental Art.

Fairservis, Walter. The Harappan Civilization and Its Writing. New Delhi: Oxford University Press.

Shendhe, Malati. The Civilized Demons: The Harappans in Rigveda. Abhinav Publications.

Chakravarty, Ranabir. Trade and Traders in Early Indian Society. New Delhi: Manohar.

Chandra, Moti. Trade and Trade Routes in Ancient India. Abhinav Publications.

Ajithprasad, P. The Pre-Harappan Cultures of Gujarat. Delhi-Manohar.

Ali, Ihsan. Early Settlements, Irrigation and Trade-Routes in Peshwar Plain, Pakistan. Frontier Archeology.

Schmmel, Marleanne. Oxford University Press.

Damodar Dharmanand Kosambi. An Introduction to the study of Indian History. Popular Prakashan Pvt. Ltd.

Ghosh, A. An Encyclopedia of Indian Archeology-Volume 1. Munshiram Manoharlal Publishers Pvt. Ltd.

Danino, Michel. The Lost River: On The Trail Of The Sarasvati. Penguin Books.

Hallo, William. Origins-Ancient Near Eastern Back ground of some Modern Western Institutions.

McIntosh, Jane. The ancient Indus Valley: New perspectives.

Kenoyer. Ancient Cities of the Indus Valley Civilization. Oxford University Press.

Barber, E.J.W. Prehistoric Textiles. Princeton University Press.

Marshall, John. Mohenjo-Daro and The Indus Civilization. Asian Educational Services.